THE RESTLESS FEW

James M. Watjen

Anuci Press

First paperback edition 2025

Anuci Press edition 2025

www.anuci-press.com

Cover Design by James M Watjen

Wrap by Adrian Medina

Fabledbeastdesign.wordpress.com

ISBN 979-8-9926529-8-7 (paperback)

THE RESTLESS FEW

ISBN 979-8-9926529-9-4(eBook)

THE RESTLESS FEW

CHAPTER ONE

"Even though I walk through the valley of the shadow of death, I will fear no evil..." Psalm 23:1-6

I had given them the forgiveness they had pleaded for when God would not entertain their requests. Their beginning and endings were all the same. From the darkness, into the darkness. It made no difference how they would plead, or what trivial excuse they would scream out, their sins had all been due to malevolent practices. Their calling was to return to the virulent cesspool they had been birthed from. Unfortunately, I was to receive their calls for penance and relieve them of their tormented past.

I spent many hours, days, and even years calling to a power that would answer with the same reply. An unspoken whisper that gave me the guidance to bring change in the face of unspeakable sins. It made no difference the sex, age, race, or any other worldly mark, God was calling me, and I could not ignore Him. I tried. I begged for

Him to give them peace by any other means, but their sins were too displeasing. He had seen enough and petitioned me to cleanse the world and to not call His decisions into question.

The search for understanding was not easy to find. I spent weeks seeking refuge in the written works of the apostles and the other authors who had divine callings. Yet, he continued to present Himself to me and was stern in His demands. On occasion, I would find myself in the most numbed state, clutching a flask that I kept on hand, leftover from a life that I had run from and never truly escaped. I begged God to let me forget the past and prevent the future. He only laughed. He had made this His will from the start.

The life I had before I was called by a higher power had been a road that twisted and curved around a car wreck of a youth and an equally chaotic early adulthood. Pieces of my memory had been scattered through time and reassembled through photographs and stories my grandparents would later recite to me. I had come to reside with my grandmother and grandfather in my early years, which were, at best, a collection of mental still frames and memorable audio snippets that had fought for residency inside the sanctuary of my mind.

Born into the arms of an unloving and unbalanced prostitute of a mother, I was thrown into a world of depravity and chaos. I was forced at a young age to fend for myself. The circumstances of my arrival were never made entirely clear to me, but from what I was able to gather through my grandparents, I was the result of a brutal attack by the hands of a potential unholy client. I was told that my mother had been working the streets of a district on the southern side of Chicago that she was not familiar with, a district that held many of society's unforgivable sinners. One of them happened to take a particular liking to her and took it upon himself to leave her with scars of an assorted variety as reminders of his fondness. It was mentioned to me that he was coined the "Maywood Madman."

According to my grandparents, just before their unfortunate passing a few years ago, my mother had escaped death after a sexual assault and was discovered with multiple slash marks across her body by a pizza delivery driver who had inadvertently gotten lost looking for his last delivery of the night. Her left hand had been savagely severed and placed by the sidewalk near her body. A mark of a devious being that only worked to serve his own desires. My mother would come to learn that she was with a child several weeks later when she woke from her medically induced coma. The result of that untimely encounter was myself, Father Thomas Abner. The attack had left her with physical, emotional, and mental damage that she would never fully recover from. An attack that *I* would never recover from.

My mother, although in the deep trenches of her own mental chaos, battled through as much as humanly possible to give me some semblance of a life. Her recovery from the attack that brought me into this world, coupled with the loss of her hand, made for a difficult situation when caring for an infant. Enter my grandparents. My mother had made the easy decision to take residence at my grandparents' home in an effort to provide me with stability, but also to keep herself from reentering the wretched world of the slums and pimps of the South Side of the Windy City. She kept a diary after my birth that outlined her difficulties adjusting to life as a mother and the stringent Catholic lifestyle of my grandparents. She would make notations within the diary of special moments we shared. None of which I remember.

My matriarch's battle on the streets followed her into the home of my grandparents, as the demons refused to let her leave them behind. The streets in southern Chicago never let anyone leave without taking a piece of them along. The years of substance abuse to curb the trauma my mother felt at the hands of her transgressor continued as we made my grandparents' house our home. She would sneak away at odd hours and only return when she had gotten her fix. She was devoted to the spirits that would rob her of the days and lead her blindly through the nights. I vaguely remembered pleading with my mother to wake up in the afternoons and my grandparents shuffling me into the other room. Hell wouldn't stop pounding at her door, no matter how many deadbolts she threw up.

My grandparents would give her daily reminders of the life she had led outside of the protection of their walls and would beg her to consider talking to the priest of our parish. Father Shaun, a young graduate of the seminary, had worked with victims of domestic violence. He had seen and converted the worst of the worst. The notion of God would sometimes curl my mother's lip, like she was disgusted at the thought of being looked at as needy. She was a proud woman. Proud of the life she had led, the life she was living, and the thought of an early grave. Live fast, die young, and leave a good-looking corpse seemed to be the motto by which she carried herself. Several times before her passing, Father Shaun would knock on our bedroom door, but only to be turned away with cursing and various items such as lamps, ashtrays, and even the Bible that my grandparents kept in each room, being flung against the door. He was persistent, but there was no breaking the hard shell that had wrapped my mother so tightly.

Father Shaun would pray almost daily with my grandparents. I would watch from the living room with a strong curiosity. They were all so committed to bringing my mother into the arms of God. This interest would push me into discussions with my grandparents, who first introduced me into the Catholic faith. They were unwavering in their faith and made sure that we attended Saturday evening mass every week. This attention to their faith became the strongest memory of my youth. Though I wanted better experiences with my mother, it was not to happen.

The memories of my mother and I were either clouded by the intense actions that led her to an early grave, and the fact that I was so young when I found her in her end state. I was only seven years old when my mother proceeded from this earth, surely being called to burn among the others that served no one but themselves. The unnerving scene of me entering into her room when she hadn't answered for a few days, only to find her pendulous body hanging over the side of the bed. Entering the room, my eyes began to bulge and fill with tears. I screamed in fear, agony, and pain. An immense pool of nearly coagulated blood had formed under her arm as blood continued to trickle from an open wound on her wrist. Her bed was disheveled and held the artifacts of a drug-fueled bender that must have pushed her to the edge.

I screamed for my grandfather, who had been working on preparing dinner downstairs. He grabbed me, pulling me tight and shielding my eyes from the horrific sight. As I peered between his fingers and back towards the bluish gray body, I gasped. Forever carved into my mind, I vividly recall a dark human-like figure sitting on the headboard of the bed. No true facial features except for two empty sockets where eyes should sit, and an uncomfortably bright smile, the smile never wavering, as I felt the terror creep inside me. I hugged my grandfather tightly as he began to drag me away into the hallway outside the room. The sinister figure refused to move from the headboard, directly above my mother, but I could sense it was staring the most dreadful stare through the dark holes in its head.

My grandfather quickly dragged me downstairs and immediately called the Lake County Sheriff's Department. My grandmother had been visiting with another member of the congregation. She returned to the house to find my mother being wheeled out on the stretcher. Her shrieks of pain echoed across the neighboring homes. The neighbors had begun to arrive and console my grandmother as she knelt in agony. Her hands folded and praying, she begged for my mother to be forgiven, for her to find peace and asylum in Heaven. I stood on the porch in a state of shock and horror, still trying to decipher that scene I had witnessed inside as Father Shaun grabbed my hand.

"Thomas, I'm so sorry for all of this. I've been praying for your mother every day since the first time we spoke," he said as he stared directly into my eyes.

I didn't say anything. I couldn't find the ability to push my breath past my vocal cords. I felt a sense of nothing as Father Shaun continued staring, his face slowly giving way to the horrible dark and faceless being I had seen in my mother's room. His look of concern slipping into that sinister smile. The discoloration of his teeth from years of coffee and tea, drifting into a bright white grim smile. The pupils of his eyes drawing into his sockets, backing away from the light and being replaced with nothing but dark holes. The terror came creeping back in as the tears began to fall from my face and meet the steps below.

"Thomas. Thomas. Thomas!" he nearly yelled as he shook me back into a state of consciousness.

Father Shaun quickly grabbed my hands and began to pray. His words were like mumbles set against the sound of an ambulance, the neighbors, and my grandparents' loud grieving. The sight of my mother, the nightmare on the bed, and the chaos unfolding were too much for my senses to register. I pulled my hands back, looked at Father Shaun, and ran to the backyard. I quickly made my way to the small playground stationed behind the house and sat on the swings. I wept till there was nothing left. No tears. No feelings. Just an empty mind and a drained soul. Looking up at the upstairs window, I noticed an outline standing at the glass. A white smile breaking through the darkness. I closed my eyes as Father Shaun began to walk towards me and sat on the grass in front of me.

"I will pray for you every day, Thomas. I will always be here for you. Please know that," he said as I opened my eyes.

I had grown used to him being there as a sign of comfort during the struggles my mother and I faced. Suddenly, a sensation I hadn't felt in so long came over me. It was as if someone had wiped the world of all the evil and terror. The tears returned as I felt my body being lifted and carried back to the front of my house and into the arms of my grandfather. His embrace was the first sense of comfort I had felt in a while as I slipped into a deep sleep. Though the memories before this point had been fragmented, the evening of my mother's passing would forever be stained across my mind. Unfortunately, there would be no holy memory of that night.

#

CHAPTER TWO

The weeks and months that followed the untimely death of my mother were blurred. When I finally came to, I was placed by the state under the care of my grandparents. They struggled with the loss just as much as I did, if not more. Their relationship with my mother had been an ebb and flow of unrequited and returned love. Through it all, they seemed to eventually find some solace in the fact that the opportunity to correct what they felt they had failed at in the past was with me. They were devout Catholics, and after the incident, began to frequent the church even more. We would visit Father Shaun at St. Christopher's twice, and occasionally three times, a week.

The Cathedral of St. Christopher was immaculate and inviting. Large arches spanned across an extremely high ceiling, while giant limestone pillars held the holy structure's roof. The huge stained-glass windows that lined the sides of the building displayed the fourteen stations of the cross and bled just enough light through to dimly illuminate the outer pews. The center held the altar and an enormous depiction of the crucifix of Jesus Christ. A statue of the Holy Mother Mary sat to the right of the walkway into the church, positioned next to the holy water fountains. It was everything that would remind you that this was a sanctuary of peace and hope.

Mass was required attendance in the household and the welcoming responsiveness of the church gave me assurance that the evils I had experienced up to this point in my life had been defeated. I would kneel on the worn and bruised leather cushions under the rickety pews and pray for the continued safety and health of my grandparents. They had given me so much more than I had expected, and I felt a duty to protect them through my faith. I became infatuated with the reality of a life after this world. A life where drugs, murderers, and all forms of corruption were absent. I had been moved by the Holy Spirit and was persuaded to help spread the word.

One Saturday afternoon after service had ended, I sat in the pew and stared up at the golden crucifix that sat at the altar. As I sat and ran through the roster of questions that I had for God, Father Shaun took a seat next to me.

"Father Shaun? Why didn't God let my momma come with me?" I would ask directly.

"Well Thomas, God's will is different for every person. You mother was trying to fight off the demons, but they dug their claws too deep. Maybe her reason for being here was to bring you here, with me. Maybe she was martyred so you could be closer to God."

"What does martyred mean?" I remembered asking with strong curiosity.

"That's kind of a difficult question to answer, Thomas. Look, when someone loves someone else so much, they make certain sacrifices for that other person. Sometimes, that sacrifice is big, very big. On certain occasions, that sacrifice is their life on earth," Father Shaun said in such a delicate manner.

"So did God take my mom with him to Heaven?" I asked, anxiously awaiting his answer.

"Thomas, I don't know the answer to that. If God's will was to have her sit with Him, then yes."

"What if that wasn't His will?" I could feel my voice start to crack as I searched for answers.

"Well, Thomas...."

I felt a hand reach down to my shoulder from the pew behind me. It was my grandfather. He had been sitting behind us and overheard the discussion. I glanced back to see a look of concern on his face shifting to a big smile.

"Thanks, Father," I said as I lowered my head and stood up.

"Thomas, don't ever be afraid to ask me anything or if you just need an ear to talk to, I will listen."

"We appreciate that very much, Father," my grandfather said as he stood up and motioned for me to leave the pew.

The brief walk back to the car felt like miles. I began to question why my grandfather was uneasy about my questions for Father Shaun. Sure, my mother was gone, but where was she now? What was God's will for me and was the end result a bright, gold-filled road to Heaven or am I pawn to push His agenda? These questions ate at me the entire drive back home. After arriving home, I started to walk inside, but my grandfather stopped me.

"Tommy, Father Shaun is a good friend. Trust me, I know. Sometimes there are things that even he doesn't know the answers to. Some things are better left unknown too," my grandfather said as he grabbed and lightly squeezed my shoulder.

This was my grandfather's way of telling me not to ask too many questions because I might not like the answers. I was able to understand this, even at such a young age. We proceeded into the kitchen where my grandmother was getting started on the evening dinner plans. She was always cooking something. It was an easy way to switch my mind towards something that I knew would be comforting. Her recipes and ability to create dishes from nothing were on par with any Michelin-star restaurant. It had been my comfort many times before and would continue to be so until her passing.

After dinner was finished, I made my way upstairs to prep for a bath. I was scheduled to go back to school the following week and knew that the routine would not return so easily. I was slow to walk up the carpeted stairs and onto the landing. My mother's room sat shut on the other end of the hallway from the bathroom, but it never got easier walking up there. As I turned left from the top of the staircase, I looked back towards the end of the hall. The door to her room was slightly cracked, and that was enough for me to move as quickly as possible to the bathroom, locking the door when it slammed shut.

I gasped for air as I sat against the old wooden door that separated me from the dimly lit landing. I felt uneasy as I began to get undress and turned the shower on. After checking the bathroom door, I crept into the shower and began to bathe. Occasionally pulling the shower curtain aside, I was relieved to see there was nothing there. My eyes remained open as the shampoo washed from my head. My eyes burning, I quickly turned to wash the soap suds away that had glazed over my eyes. I started to turn the water off and reached outside the shower for my towel. Suddenly, I felt a hand grab my arm and begin to pull.

"Tommy, help me! Save me, Tommy!" I heard as my body froze at the horror of hearing my mother's voice.

I quickly pulled the curtain back as the hair on my arms and neck began to rise. A black figure with thin black hair draped to the floor stood, with its slender fingertip pointed directly at me, motionless. I couldn't move. It had become impossible to move, to speak, or look away. It drew its finger back in a motioning fashion. There was nothing there. No eyes. No mouth. No soul. My body's flight, fight, or freeze response took over for what felt like an eternity. I searched my mind for what I was looking at, but I could not make sense of it. I snapped from my nearly catatonic state and began to scream, searching for something to hit the dark being with. Then, without reason, the lights began to flicker off and on. The being that had been standing before me was gone between the lights flashing.

"Tommy! Tommy! You alright? Unlock the door!" my grandfather yelled as he beat on the bathroom door.

I sat down in the tub and began crying as my grandparents burst through the door, covering me in a towel and lifting me from the tub. The embrace of my grandfather was a warmth like I had never experienced.

"You're alright, kiddo?" My grandfather's voice brought me the greatest feeling of comfort I had ever felt.

I spent the next weeks' time huddling next to my grandparents in their bed. Their concern had grown immensely since the bathroom episode, and they made it a point to schedule a meeting with Father Shaun to talk. I distinctly remembered leaving that day for St. Christopher's Cathedral and thinking to myself that I would probably sound insane if I described what I had seen. I prayed the whole way to the doors of the church. Upon opening the doors, we were greeted by Father Shaun and another priest who I had never met.

"Good morning, Thomas. This is Father Bristol. He works with a lot of the youth in our parish and will be joining us today. Is that alright with you?" Father Shaun asked with an overwhelmingly comforting tone.

"Sure, that's fine," I said, my voice cracking due to my lack of saliva.

"Good deal! Let's head back to the chambers and talk for a little bit. You can tell us everything you saw."

I followed the two priests back behind the altar area and through a large wooden door that looked like something out of a picture book about knights and dragons. A castle door. A door meant to ward off any unwanted attendees from entering.

"Have a seat, Thomas. So, how are you feeling today? Anything specific you want to talk about?" Father Shaun said with an intense and interested gaze.

"Well, it might sound crazy, but there is something that has been bothering me," I said in a near whisper with my head tilted and looking at the ground.

"Tell us about it, Thomas. Tell us what you saw."

#

CHAPTER THREE

"...some will abandon the faith and follow deceiving spirits and things taught by demons." 1 Timothy 4:1

I began to describe to them the nightmares I was experiencing when I was awake. The recollection of those horrible scenes, raising the hair on the back of my neck, drew their interest immediately. I watched them as they began to take notes inside of small pads of paper. They scribbled with intensity as I spoke about the shadow figures I had been encountering and the terrifying situation in the bathroom.

"When did these visions start, Thomas?" Father Bristol asked as he stared into my eyes.

"I saw the first one with my mom. I... I don't know what it was. It just kept smiling at me."

"Did it say anything to you?" Father Bristol continued as his pen shifted on the paper.

"No. It just sat there," I said as I remembered the intense scene that evening.

"What about the woman in the bathroom? Did she say anything to you?" Father Shaun asked.

"No. She didn't say anything, either."

The two priests sat with eager intentions. They wanted to hear something from the shadowy figures, but there wasn't anything to hear. Silence. That was the calling card of the visions. The creatures I had seen didn't even let a breath leave their bodies. They were there in a physical sense, but nothing audibly.

"Why do you think these shadow people are here?" Father Bristol continued with the questioning.

"I don't know. I think they want to take me away."

"Where to, Thomas?" The comforting voice of Father Shaun quickly turned to concern.

"Somewhere bad. I feel like they want to hurt me. Like they don't like me very much." I could feel my voice start to break as the emptiness from those memories began to flood my mind again.

"Why would they want to do that, Thomas?" asked Father Shaun as he held his breath.

"Maybe it's because I'm not supposed to be here? I think they took my mom somewhere, and they want me, too."

"Thomas, I honestly don't know why they are visiting you, but you were meant to be here. We will do whatever we have to do in order to make these monsters leave you alone. I promise you." Leaning in and grabbing my shoulder, Father Shaun brought me a moment of peace. I trusted him.

The meeting ending, we sat in prayer and both the priests asked God for my protection. My breath held for the entire prayer, as a personal ritual. I had hoped that my prayer would be answered, and the shadowy beings would disappear. We sat up from our chairs as my grandparents made their way into the room. I watched as they all walked to the other end of the room near an old oak desk adorned with a large crucifix on the front of it. I knew what they were talking about but couldn't make out the words, as they would all occasionally glance over. In near unison, they all turned towards me, my grandfather walking over and giving me a hug and motioning that it was time to leave.

Riding home, I could sense there was concern among my grandparents. Typically, they would be very talkative, but they were uncomfortably silent the entire drive. Something had been discussed, and I was not to know. Was it to keep the creatures from knowing? Was it too horrible an answer to tell me? I was plagued by questions over the following days, with no answers given. I felt the constant anxiety fall over me each day I was awakened in a near sweat, with no resolution to the horrible things I had talked about. Then came the reason for the harsh silence.

"Tommy, when you get dressed, come downstairs. Grandma and I wanna talk to you about something," my grandfather said as he leaned into my bedroom door that morning.

"Sure thing, Grandpa," I muttered as I wiped the thick layer of sleep from my eyes.

I had no clue what was waiting for me, given that it was early on a Saturday morning, and I had not had breakfast. Throwing my clothes on, I started across the landing with my eyes glued to the closed door that had once housed my mother. I had made my way to the landing when I saw both Father Shaun and Father Bristol seated in the living room with my grandparents. The concerned looks and concentrated stares as I entered brought my already high anxiety to a near climax. I knew that they had a resolution in mind for what I had been experiencing, but even that resolution did not please them.

"Good morning, Thomas. Hope you slept well. I brought Father Bristol along this morning because we wanted to talk to you about what you have been going through." Father Shaun always had a way of making the worst discussions seem somewhat heartening.

"Look, Thomas. After talking over the notes we made and discussing it with your grandparents, we feel that there might be a certain spirit lingering." Father Bristol was straight to the point as small sweat beads clung to his eyebrows.

"Like a bad spirit? Like a demon?" I asked with my eyes scanning across the room for answers.

"Thomas, I know it sounds crazy, but the description you gave us is a near identical match to the description another child gave, who experienced similar circumstances a few years ago. Father Bristol was able to save the soul of that child and can help us to help you." The voice of Father Shaun nearly cracked as he turned a pleading gaze at me.

"I dunno. I mean, they haven't really hurt me or anything," I quietly replied.

The room sat in silence for what felt like ten minutes, but it was only for a single minute. I could hear the sound of my own heart begin to pump more furiously through the still yet unnerved room. I began to look around the room for reassurance that there were other answers to be found but was met with blank stares.

"This probably sounds like an extreme answer, but after talking with everyone, we think it might be best if we schedule a time to perform some special prayers. It'll just be Father Bristol and me in the room and your grandparents will be right outside the door."

"Oh, okay. Why can't my grandparents be in the room, too?" I asked as I held my breath.

"Well, Thomas, the room needs to have only the holiest of individuals in the room. Your grandparents are fantastic members of the church and will be praying outside of the room. We just need to make sure that if any of those bad spirits show up again, they won't try and hurt you or your grandparents. The Lord won't let anything happen to you. We won't let anything happen to you." Father Shaun's bolstering gave me a sense of peace.

"Will it make them stay away? Like, forever?" I asked.

"Thomas, you and I both know that when the Lord is with us in that room, they won't be coming back. Ever." The reassurance from Father Bristol was convincing.

"But what if the thing I saw in the bathroom wasn't evil? What if it was trying to tell me something? What if it was my mom?" I asked in a near shout.

"Tommy, that's enough!" my grandfather yelled in a stern voice.

"I know the loss of your mom was hard, Thomas. Believe me, I know, but what you saw wasn't your mother. We both know that she wouldn't try to scare you like that or even hurt you. Your mom is in a better place," Father Shaun said in the calmest of tones as he held back any tears trying to make their way out.

"But Father Shaun, what if she isn't in a better place? What if it's God's will for her to come back to be with me?" I asked with the highest of hope that I had the right answer, but the mood in the room quickly became somber.

My grandmother grabbed her mouth as tears began to flow down her cheeks. She stood up and began to walk out towards the dining room as my grandfather grabbed me and hugged me tighter than he had ever done. Tighter than the night my mother had left this earth for another calling. For the briefest moment, the world was on pause, and I didn't feel any pain. However, it wasn't to last forever. I would chase any opportunity to feel that way again, even if it took me to Hell.

#

CHAPTER FOUR

"Jesus rebuked the unclean spirit, and healed the child, and delivered him again to his father." Luke 9:42

The following days were spent in a near automated fashion as I waited for news of what was to be my relief from the shadows that lurked around me. I went through the normal motions, and it almost felt as if the day would never come. Then, without a single preemptive warning, the day came. We were seated in the living room, watching a rerun of a popular children's show titled *Lucy's Playground,* when the doorbell rang. The silence that came over the room and the still, cold air cut through me as my grandfather slowly stood up and shuffled towards the door. Light flooded the entry way and through the light stepped Father Shaun and Father Bristol, both carrying small briefcases.

"Good morning, Mr. and Mrs. Abner. Thomas," Father Shaun greeted us as the light from the entry way gave way to darkness when the door shut.

"Do any of you have any questions or any concerns that we can address before we get started?" Father Bristol clearly presented the question with the intent to be hit by a flood of questions, but there was only dead air.

"Nothing? Well then, should we go ahead to the room?" Father Shaun said with a nervousness to his voice that told me this could become painful. His hands folded as he awaited directions from my grandfather.

I slowly stood up, my grandmother standing with me and doing her best to comfort me by rubbing my shoulder, but the uneasy tension was spreading rapidly. The two priests grabbed their briefcases and followed my grandfather up the stairs. My grandmother and I followed behind with great hesitance. Upon reaching the landing, we moved towards the room that my mother had occupied and eventually met her ending inside.

The door creaked open, and I could feel my head begin to spin. I didn't want to go in there, but I was reassured that there would be nothing to hurt me. Still, the memory of seeing my deceased mother dangling from the bed was cooked inside my mind to the point that the heat traveled through my veins and into the pit of my stomach. I briefly held back the nausea until my breakfast was boiling over inside me. I quickly grabbed the trash can from inside the doorway and began to vomit.

The pain from the intense session of vomiting caused the whites of my eyes to be glazed over with blood as the vessels inside my eyeballs exploded, leaving me with a near zombified appearance. The look of concern on Father Shaun's face as I pulled my head back from the trash can and revealed my drooling and red eyes brought on an entirely new fear. A fear of something that I would not understand till later. The fear of the most unholy.

"Thomas! Are you alright? This is clearly the work of a demonic spirit that does not want us here! We are not leaving, you Hell-bound heathen! Do you hear me!" Father Bristol screamed as he lifted his fist to the sky in a fit of rage.

Father Shaun proceeded to lead me to the bed and instructed my grandparents to leave the room as they would soon begin the process of sending the evil spirits that had been plaguing me back to their wicked world. My grandparents each gave me a kiss on the forehead and walked towards the door, making a sign of the cross on their chests as they looked back at me.

"Thomas, we're going to lock the door for your safety and ours as well. If you don't mind, we're going to move the standing mirror to the front of the bed. This is just a safety procedure in case the evil spirits try and flee," Father Bristol calmly assured me as he wheeled the mirror from the corner of the room to the front of the bed.

I watched as Father Shaun sat his briefcase on the end of the bed and opened it to reveal a plethora of items meant to return the demon to its place in Hell. He began to set the items on the end table beside the bed. A small vile of water that was adorned by a crucifix, a Holy Bible with the cover text outlined in gold, a wooden crucifix, complete with a porcelain body of Jesus Christ dripping blood, a small, opened box of tissues, a leather-bound black notebook, and a sharpened number two pencil. All items meant to send the worst spirits to retreat to their unholiest of lairs.

The priests requested that I lay down on the bed, as to not fall off in the event that the spirits began to throw my body from the wooden bed frame. I obliged. Staring at the ceiling and counting the lines between the tiles to draw my attention from what was occurring, I caught Father Bristol moving to the end of the bed as Father Shaun shifted to the right side of me. I could feel my anxiety elevate and my breath begin to grow more rapid.

I hadn't moved a muscle but the sweat leaking from my body and dampening the sheets would lead anyone else to believe that I had run a marathon. I had run for miles, but those miles were tracked only in my thoughts of what was going to happen. I was winded.

"Thomas, we are about ready to begin. I promise you that we will not let anything happen to you. We will be right here, and your grandparents are on the other side of the door. Are you ready?" Father Shaun said with the most certain of looks in his eyes.

I nodded. I was ready for this to be over and ready for it to continue, at the same time. Either way, I wanted answers. They wanted the same. We were all looking for the beginning of the end.

The holy water hitting my body felt cool against my sweat-covered skin. Father Bristol began to pray as he flung the water across my face and body. Constantly making the sign of a cross, his intent to rid me of my spiritual passenger was fierce. I closed my eyes as the prayers began to rise in volume. I lay in the bed motionless as they continued to harass and entice whatever had been following me, but my body felt empty. I felt nothing. No uncomfortable scraping across my body, no scramble from another being to flee. It was silent inside me, just as silent as it had been before.

Father Shaun lifted the crucifix into the air and began to plead with the demons to run. He began to pray with an intent that made you aware of his end goal. The prayers continued on for several minutes, and then a brief pause. The cross now placed on the bed, he slowly picked up the notebook and began to inscribe every detail of what had happened and what was still happening. He looked at Father Bristol and then back at me as a silence floated down through the room like a dense fog.

"Everything alright in there, Father?" my grandfather shouted from outside the door.

"Thomas, do you feel anything? What do you see?"

I sat up and looked around, not feeling any different from what I had felt when the ceremony had started.

"Nothing. Nothing happened. I don't feel like anything changed," I stated in a near frustrated manner.

"Everything is fine, Mr. Abner. Just a little while longer, please?" Father Bristol shouted back.

The concern in the eyes and demeanor of the priests meant one of two things. Either their lack of experience in exorcisms had been noticed by the shadows that lived inside me, and it was a wasted attempt, or the unwelcome beings had decided to flee before the first prayers were uttered. I grabbed the notepad that the reverend had set on the bed and began to doodle on one of the blank pages. They were discussing their results at the foot of the bed, each of them in a state of confusion, possibly tricked into questioning their own faith. I began to draw one of the shadow figures I had previously witnessed the day my mother had passed. It was almost as if the motions were not of my own.

"Thomas. Thomas, what is that? What are you drawing?" Father Shaun said as he walked to the bedside. Father Bristol was frozen and leaning over the footing of the bed in a state of shock.

"It's the dark man. He was the first one. He wasn't welcome here."

I dragged the pencil back and stared at the drawing of a silhouette of a dark shadowy figure. A huge gaping grin filled with white canine-like fangs. Something had compelled me, but I couldn't place it. I looked up at Father Bristol's shock-ridden face, his eyes glued to the paper. I looked up at the mirror that was next to Father Bristol. I began to cry as the reflection displayed the large, dark, shadowy figure seated behind me in the bed. No eyes. No sound. No soul. A figure that smiled and nothing more.

I quickly turned around to catch a glimpse of the unwelcome figure behind me. Nothing. I quickly turned back to see it still sitting in the reflection and pointing towards me. I repeated this action as my voice froze and the tears began to flow from my cheeks.

"Thomas! What is it? Tell me! What do you see?" Father Shaun begged as he lifted the crucifix and began to pray as quickly as he could. his breath leaving his body quicker than the words from his mouth.

"Is it him, Thomas? Thomas! What is he doing? Please speak to me!"

I was in shock. I couldn't move, my body frozen and staring into the black holes that provided nothing in return. There was no expression apart from that damned smile. I could feel the anger beginning to rise up as the figure began to nod his head. Silently, the figure's arm extended from the mirror and began to reach out for Father Bristol, its dark and slender fingers growing in the length like claws extending as it closed in on the neck of the unsuspecting elder priest.

There was a tremendous rage inside that demanded I stop the beast. I grabbed the pencil, drawing it back and above my head. I closed my eyes as I brought the pencil down into a fleshy mound in front of me. Opening my eyes, I was horrified to see the pencil stuck between the shoulder blade and neck of Father Bristol. He screamed in agony as he grabbed the pencil and removed it with a strong pull, knocking the mirror over and shattering it in a painful fit.

"What's going on in there?" my grandfather screamed as he began to beat on the door.

Father Shaun quickly ran to Father Bristol as he lay writhing in pain. The door quickly burst open, my grandparents rushing into the room, my grandmother running to console me as I began to sob in terror over what I had done. My grandfather assisted with standing Father Bristol up.

"It was him! He was trying to grab you! I swear it!" I managed to yell as my voice continued to break.

"It's alright, Thomas. It's alright. We'll get Father Bristol to the hospital. I will be back. I promise," Father Shaun said as he and my grandfather lifted the injured priest to his feet and began to carry him out.

I laid my head on my grandmother's lap and cried myself to sleep as she ran her hands through my hair. A sleep that wouldn't bring rest but a momentary sense of peaceful lapse in memory. The unwelcome wouldn't find me there.

#

CHAPTER FIVE

"Whoever is righteous has regard for the life of his beast, but the mercy of the wicked is cruel. Proverbs 12:10

Several days had passed before I learned that Father Bristol was recovering at home. My eyes had become dry from the non-stop crying and the constant scanning of the room for any of the figures. I was certain at this point that they would be back if I did not keep my surroundings in check. The emotional attachment between myself and the quiet beings had drained me like a leech on an open wound. My eyes were surrounded by dark circles that would make a black hole seem a tint too bright. I slept, or rather, rested when the lingering uneasiness would become too much. It brought my grandparents much pain to now see their grandchild slowly drifting, much like his mother had. Perhaps she had seen them, too? Were they the catalyst that had driven her to searching for a way out, even if that meant eternally sedating herself?

After the incident with the priests, my grandparents were relentless in their search for answers about my visions. They would regularly question me, asking if I had seen any of the creatures. Locking doors, putting sharp objects up high, and checking on my well-being became the norm. They slowly began to relent as the answer continued to be no. A few weeks had passed, and my grandparents were convinced that the worst had subsided, deciding that returning to school would be the next best course of action.

I had been attending a local private Catholic school that was overseen by the St. Christopher's diocese before the incident involving my late mother. The school had been very forgiving regarding my recent absence, but my classmates, not so much. Prior to the death and visions, my school life had been very average. Grades were good, friends were plenty, and the teachers understanding. Upon returning, I soon realized that the innocence of the other children in my class had dissipated and been replaced with the opposite end of the spectrum. Cruelty.

The days that followed my return were met with awkward stares. Forced to sit at the cafeteria table alone and devoid of interaction with almost all the other children. Even the teachers gave an off-putting glare when I entered the classrooms. The silent whispers among the other students quickly gave way to an avalanche of insults and verbal harassment that would bury the most mentally stable.

They would pass papers containing depictions of shadows all over the page, making sure that the visuals would make their way to my seat. Only one other student, a quiet and seemingly friendly young girl who had recently moved to our school, had shown me any compassion.

Eleanor had moved to our area from an east coast city in New Jersey with her family. Her father had taken a job that oversaw the local public transit in the southernmost side of Chicago, an area that had suffered from extreme crime and poverty longer than I had existed. She quickly became a protector of sorts, making sure that I had someone to sit and talk with at the lunch tables. Her defense of the weak extended far past myself, and eventually she was respected among the other students.

"Thomas, don't worry about them. They don't know shit about anything," Eleanor would remind me almost daily.

Her language and how she carried herself spoke volumes about a less-than-quiet home life. Eleanor had no tolerance for bullying, and she made it known to the other students. Being the youngest sibling in a family of six, Eleanor knew how to carry herself when it came to the other students.

"Eleanor, why did you decide to talk to me?" I remembered asking her.

"Because no one else was, Thomas. Those other kids have it too easy. They get to go home and not see or hear anything but the love of their parents. Us, though? We gotta stick together."

I didn't understand but I knew what she meant, all at the same time. Eleanor was the first real comfort I had felt outside of my grandparents. Her strength was enough to prop up a collapsing building, or even a collapsing youth like myself.

"Do you know why they look at me like that?" I quietly asked her during one of our lunch table conversations, butting in as she talked about the latest episode of one our favorite shows, *Lucy's Playground*.

"Yeah. Yeah, I know why, but I don't mind it," she replied with some hesitation.

"What did they tell you?" I asked in hopes that what she knew was a lie.

She stared at the lunch table for a few moments, as if she was searching through an invisible note of all the right things to say. "They said you stabbed Father Bristol. They said you see monsters," Eleanor whispered as she slowly glanced around the lunch room.

"Anything else?" I questioned, as I wanted to make sure that it was the only piece of information she was aware of.

"Yeah, Thomas," she replied with a distant stare past my shoulder into oblivion.

"Eleanor, what else did they say?" I needed more answers.

"Nothing, Thomas. It wasn't anything." she said as she held steadfast in her answer, but I knew there was more.

Our friendship continued to grow and soon, the whispers and uncomfortable gazes from the other students started to die down. Everything had seemed fine for months, until one of the older kids, a brute of an eighth grader in the class above ours had discovered who I was and what had happened. We would pass each other in the hall, and he would hold a rubberneck as I passed by. He was waiting for the perfect time, and he would eventually find it. A warm and bright Friday afternoon in the spring, at the age of nine years old, I would come face-to-face with him.

Children could be so cruel.

#

CHAPTER SIX

"Rescue the weak and the needy; deliver them from the hand of the wicked." Psalm 82:4

I was waiting for the bus around back of the old school annex, a dilapidated building where typing class and music would take place in the afternoons. As I sat and waited for the bus, a shadow appeared on the ground ahead of me. Not like the other shadows I had previously seen, but one of much greater width that was followed with a shove to my upper back. Lurching forward, I quickly turned around to see the hulking figure of the older eighth grader standing in front of me.

"So, you're that chicken-shit tough kid, huh? The one that sees dead people?" he said with a smirk widening across his face.

"I don't... I don't know what you mean," I quietly muttered.

"Yeah, you do. You're the one that caught Father Bristol by surprise. You gave him a good stab, didn't you? You think you're pretty tough, huh?" he continued as he moved towards me.

"I didn't mean—"

"Your druggy mom teach you how to be so tough? Oh wait, that's not possible, is it? A dead druggy can't teach anything, can they?" His steps were closing in and his voice was gaining in volume.

I felt a fire begin to burn inside as his insults continued. A good shove sent me to the ground as he stood lurching over me. As the anger began to rise up, a figure behind him caught my eye.

"Get up! Why don't you try me like you did Father Bristol, you little shit!" he yelled as he began to lean over, grabbing my collar and drawing his hand back.

As he brought his clinched fist back, he could see the terror in my eyes. His smile had nearly encompassed his entire face. Then he noticed I wasn't looking at him. I was staring at an equally enormous dark figure standing directly behind him. Its smile broke through the darkness filling my vision as it pointed at me.

"What are you looking at, asshole? I'm talking to you! Look at me when I'm talking to you!" he screamed out as he looked in every direction for what my eyes were fixed on.

I closed my eyes and began to pray. I whispered, peeking through the small slit between my eyelids, as he stood there in confusion. He pulled his fist back, but was unexpectedly sent to the ground, holding the back of his head.

"Get the fuck off him, jerk!"

My eyes quickly opened as Eleanor grabbed me by the arm and brought me to my feet. She was standing with a large rock in one hand and my arm secured tightly in the other.

"What the fuck is wrong with you? You think it's cool to pick on younger kids?" she shrieked at the eighth grader, who was now cowering and holding the back of his head. A small lesion on the back of his head had left a few drops of blood leaking between his fingers.

"If you got a problem with Thomas, then you've got a problem with me! Do you understand, fuckhead?"

"Yea...yeah. I understand. Just put that rock down. I'm done," the eighth grader replied as he slowly came to his feet, the other kids around him covering their mouths and holding back the laughter at what had just taken place.

"Come on, Tommy. We're going home," Eleanor, helping to brush my pants off, said with a glare at the injured eighth grader.

We broke through the small crowd that had formed and began to walk in the opposite direction. That day would forever be embedded in my memory and linger vividly for years to come. The walk home felt like it took forever, even though it was only about ten blocks from the school. Rounding the corner to my house, I looked up at Eleanor in near tears. She could tell the damage was done. Not physically, but emotionally.

"Thomas, you can't let those assholes get to you like that. You gotta stand up for yourself. Don't let them talk to you like that. They don't know shit about you, and sometimes you have to remind them." Eleanor had obviously dealt with a similar scenario before because her voice was almost motherly.

"Here. I want you to have this. My grandmother gave this to me after my mom died. It's a protector charm. It'll help keep those assholes away and maybe those other things," Eleanor said, pulling a necklace over her head.

Opening my palm, she placed the necklace in my hand and closed it.

"It's kept me safe, but I think you'll need it more than me now. Anyhow, I don't think that asshole is going to be bothering me or you after today." She laughed as she turned away.

"Thanks," I garbled as she looked back.

"I'll see you tomorrow, Tommy?"

"Yeah, I'll see you tomorrow," I replied as I turned and continued walking towards my home.

Stepping onto the porch, I opened my hand to see what Eleanor had given me. It was a shiny gold charm on a gold necklace. It held an engraving of a man walking with a large stick and a child posted securely on his shoulder.

"St. Christopher Protect Us" was embossed around the figure of the man and the child. I slowly opened the necklace and draped it over my head. Gripping the charm tight, I gave it a kiss of reverence as I stepped into the house.

#

CHAPTER SEVEN

"And then many will fall away and betray one another and hate one another." Matthew 24:10

The following weeks leading to the end of school were the most casual of weeks. No stares. No glances over the shoulder. The world seemed to be on the mend, and I was back to being a shadow in a room full of talking bodies. Eleanor and I began to hang out almost daily. We were quickly becoming the best of friends. A friendship that would last through the next several years as we pushed forward into high school.

This moment in my life was among the happiest I had ever experienced. I had a friend outside of my home that I could confide in. Someone who would listen and not judge me based on my past. I learned more and more about Eleanor and how she had been given up for adoption at birth, only to be rescued by a family that had once been of wealthy stature and who would later lose it via her father's gambling addiction.

Her mother had made the decision to run off with another man, leaving her to fend for her and her father. His decision to move to the Southside of Chicago was an attempt to start over and rectify his past transgressions. In my eyes, he had done so by bringing Eleanor into my life.

Things were going great. We would spend the afternoons discussing books and films we were reading, the latest gossip going around school, and what our plans were after we made it through high school. With everything going so well, I would not have expected the sudden jolt of sadness that would soon impact me in my senior year of high school. I had gone the past several years without another incident, and I had even begun therapy with a local therapist. None of that mattered one afternoon, when I arrived home to the most dreadful of news.

I had just walked in the door when I discovered my grandmother sobbing uncontrollably at the kitchen table. I dropped my bag at the doorway and quickly ran to comfort her and discover why she was so upset.

"It's alright, Granny. Tell me what happened. Where's Grandpa?" I questioned her as I wrapped my arms around her, holding her tightly as she cried on my shoulder.

"Thomas, I'm so sorry. I'm so sorry," she quietly said as the tears flowed down her cheeks and onto the table below, her head now in her hands.

"Where's Grandpa, Granny?"

Continuing to search for comfort in the most terrible of times, I ran to the living room, my hand quickly lifting to cover my mouth as I saw it. A grisly scene of my grandfather sprawled on the ground, blood leaking into a pool that saturated his blue and white striped shirt. A gaping wound on the side of his head displayed the beige coloration of his skull. My head began to spin as I braced my back against the doorframe and slid down. I sat in horror as I felt the cold come through the house, the sound of an ambulance pulsating in the distance.

"He fell, Thomas. I tried to wake him up and he wouldn't. I called the ambulance and Father Shaun. I didn't know what to do. I'm so sorry," my grandmother cried out.

The glare of the sun was shining through the living room and the reflection from the old wooden television cabinet pushed the bright light into my eyes. I shielded them and, looking to my right and down the hallway, I saw it. It was staring. Not moving or even smiling like before. It had come back for me.

"Get the fuck away from me, you bastard!" I screamed out down the hall as I stood up, wiping the tears and snot from my face.

"Thomas, what is it?" my grandmother asked, showing concern that someone was in the house.

"You did this! This is your fault! Fuck you!" The scream carried down the hallway in the direction of the figure, but there was no movement.

I quickly began to pray, closing my hand around the charm that Eleanor had given me years past. The necklace had never left my neck since I had received it that day. I stared at the murky figure and began to move forward. It stepped backwards, deeper into the darkness behind it. I continued to pray, louder with each step, as the beast began to smile and raise its finger, motioning me to step closer.

"Thomas!" I heard the familiar voice yell out from behind me.

"Father?" I muttered as I turned around.

The light peering around Father Shaun made him look like an illuminated holy being. He slowly walked up to me and brought me close with a hug. I attempted to hold back the tears, but there was no use as his presence brought a sense of relief.

"Did you see it, Thomas?" he asked quietly into my ear, so as to not alarm my grandmother.

"It's here. It...it was in the doorway to that bedroom." I pointed down the hall.

"Alright, alright. Let's step back into the kitchen and be with your grandmother," Father Shaun whispered as he stared into the dark entrance to the bedroom.

I turned and immediately went to comfort my grandmother. The door to the outside opened as EMTs and several police arrived. We cried together as the paramedics began to tend to my grandfather's deceased body on the floor.

"I'm so sorry, Denise. Hank was a great man. He is with our Lord and savior today. I'm here if either of you need anything."

"Thank you, Father. I just can't believe it. I...I was in the back room folding laundry when I heard him fall. I didn't know what to do," my grandmother stammered as her words cut through the tears.

"You did everything right. I understand this is an awful thing, but please find solace in knowing that he now sits at the foot of our father in Heaven. I'm here if you need anything."

We sat and watched as the group of medical staff lifted my grandfather onto the stretcher. The coroner had arrived and began to assess the situation. He lifted his stethoscope up to my grandfather and searched for any sign of life. Nothing. Just a cold corpse where a strong and faithful man had once been. They brought the sheet over him and began to wheel him out as my grandmother cried out a horrible shriek. I grabbed her tightly while Father Shaun prayed over the body as it left the house.

It must have been not long after he was stretchered out that the neighbors and other family members began to arrive, consoling my grandmother in her moment of frailty. I made my way to the phone near the pantry door and quickly dialed Eleanor's number. It rang, yet no answer. I called again. Still there was no response on the other end. The neighbors had surrounded my grandmother as I made the impulse decision to drive over to Eleanor's home, just a few blocks over from ours.

Eleanor opened the door after several repeated knocks and doorbell rings. She was surprised but could immediately sense that something was wrong.

"Thomas? What's wrong? Are you alright?" she questioned as she stepped outside the door and onto the porch.

"I saw it. It came back," I replied with my eyes glazed from grief.

I explained to her in great detail what had happened and how the dark being had appeared to be motioning for me to follow it. I told her about finding my grandmother hysterical and the grisly scene of my grandfather's accident. She simply stared at me with a worried look that said a million things, but nothing was spoken.

"Thomas, you need to go home. Your grandmother needs you right now. I'm sorry, Thomas. I think you need to talk to someone about what you're seeing, too. Have you looked into seeing a new therapist possibly?" Eleanor was cautious to say, but the words were already spoken.

"You think I'm crazy, don't you? Don't you!?" I shouted at the top of my lungs. I felt a betrayal that cut deep into my core.

"No, Thomas. I just think that—"

"I know what you think! You're just like the others! I know what I saw, damn it! It was right in front of me!" The boiling of my blood had reached a threshold that I hadn't felt in such a long time.

"Thomas, you're scaring me. I think you should leave." The fear in Eleanor's voice was real. Her once reassuring being was replaced by an insincere monster.

I turned and walked back to my car, throwing open the door as I turned to see Eleanor visibly shaken from the interaction. I stepped in and threw the car into drive and sped back to the house. My mind was swerving as my car maintained a straight destination. How could someone I trusted so much be so insistent that I was crazy? Was she really concerned or was she just like the bully behind the school annex? The thoughts began to bite down on my mind as I pulled into the carport that stood on the rear of my grandparents' home. I knew what I had seen. I knew what had been standing there. I was certain that everything I knew outside of those things was a lie.

The doorway into the kitchen was silent as I walked back into the house. A note was planted on the kitchen table.

Thomas, I'm going over to Theresa's house next door. Please let me know when you make it back. I'm worried about you. Love you, Grandma.

I sat at the kitchen table and began to cry uncontrollably. The awful scene of my grandfather's body on the floor, my grandmother crying, the thing in the doorway, and Eleanor's reaction had been too much for one afternoon. The abandonment and hopeless feeling I was experiencing crushed me with the weight of all Heaven and Hell combined. I grabbed the saintly emblem around my neck and prayed. I prayed for everything to cease. I screamed out and slammed my hand against the table.

While sitting and weeping, I felt a hand on my shoulder. I turned to look around and nothing. I jumped up. Was it that thing in the doorway again? Had it returned to take me, now that I was alone? I scanned the room, clinching my fists and waiting for it to lurch from behind any open doorway. It was at this moment that I made the decision to make my way over to my grandmother at the neighbor's house. The risk of being alone had grown to be too much.

Entering the house, I immediately felt the warm embrace of my grandmother. She held me as we wept. I felt the exhaustion creep in, and the world grew dim. I began to fall asleep in my grandmother's arms, just like I had all those years ago. The warm embrace. The lasting embrace.

#

CHAPTER EIGHT

"And let us not grow weary of doing good, for in due season we will reap, if we do not give up." Galatians 6:9

The blur of the following years finally came into focus as I was finishing my final year at the seminary. I had found serenity within the confides of the school, learning everything between Genesis and Revelation within the Holy Bible. The seminary became my refuge during my stay there, and I had all but forgotten the evil that had tormented me in my youth, both physically and spiritually.

The calling came after the death of my grandfather and at the plea of my grandmother. Her devout love for the Lord had grown even stronger after our patriarch had gone to be amongst the angels. I would spend my days studying prayers and assisting the local priests in the diocese with service. I had finally been relieved of the torment that had plagued me for so long.

The final year at St. John's Seminary required us to take on an extracurricular form of witness. I was chosen to be the chaplain at a local prison, where the worst of the worst were put to spend the rest of their days. I would lead Bible studies, assist with personal discussions that related to spirituality, and even perform last rites for those preparing to be executed.

The position required me to have security officers present, but most of the time, they would occupy themselves elsewhere and allow me one-on-one time with the prisoners. It was in these conversations that I would not only be educated about the terrible things the prisoners had done, but also, the best way to do them without getting easily caught.

The most interesting of the prisoners I met was a young man, affectionately known amongst prison staff as, The Handy Man. The respect he carried from his cellmates told me everything I needed to know about his past. He was quiet and reserved. His sunken eyes and always chapped lips were signs of his deteriorating mental health. The cell was clean, not even a speck of dirt could be found anywhere.

"Hello, Alex. I'm Father Thomas Abner."

Nothing but silence. The rattle of keys from the guards above echoed through the gray walls of the prison chambers.

"I understand that you're going through a difficult time. Maybe I can help you get through this. Are you Catholic, by chance?"

A motionless Alex Fulmer sat quietly, staring at the walls. Not even a blink of his eyes as I listened to the sound of my heart beat faster and my breathing gain volume.

"Why are you scared, Father?"

"I'm sorry?" I responded with a curious fear.

"You're breathing awfully hard. Did you do something, Father?" Alex questioned as he continued to stare at the blank walls.

"I'm not sure I follow. What do you mean, exactly?" I continued as the nervousness intensified.

The scar-ridden lips went from a flat and motionless stance to a smirk. A smirk that gave way to a look of scrutiny.

"Did the warden tell you why I'm here? Being a man of God, you shouldn't have anything to fear, unless..."

"Yes, Alex. The warden told me exactly why you are here. He told me about the horrible things you did to those who chose to inflict terrible pain on God's children. That's why I am here. I want to speak to you about it."

His face lit up like a Christmas tree in the darkest of rooms. His smirk lowered, his eyes not fixated on me or the walls but rather, wandering around the room for answers to the questions in his head.

"Well, what do you want to know, Father?"

"Everything, Alex. Every detail that you want to confess. I'm here to bring you the peace that you are looking for. No judgement, either."

We sat in the cell together. He spoke of all the horrific acts he had committed, and I listened. He told stories of how he was able to find the pedophiles and how he was able to dispose of them. He told me of the dreams he had had that were crushed by a television director. He even shed a tear when talking about his father and the events leading up to his mother's death. The chaos in his words and the isolation in his voice left me nearly speechless.

"I'm so, so sorry, Alex, that you had to endure that. God will surely give you the forgiveness you are deserved."

In a near instant, his demeanor shifted back, and his glare returned to the wall in front of him.

"Tell me something, Alex. Did you ever see anything strange when you killed these people?"

"Like what?"

"I don't know, any unusual figures? Like, shadows?" I began to search for answers.

"No. I never saw anything but their dead fucking bodies on the ground."

"Oh, alright. Well, I believe our time today is over. Should we meet again?"

"I dunno. I don't think God has much time left for me, Father," Alex said with a strong confidence.

I stood there, as I could see any hope he had left in his sunken eyes came cascading out in a blank stare. His demeanor almost immediately went back to the quiet and uncomfortable gaze of the light gray walls in front of him.

"Alex, it might not mean anything, but I believe God's purpose for you was fulfilled. Perhaps he placed you on this earth to protect those children. Maybe the method wasn't in the plans, but the end result was always going to be the same. I think the forgiveness your father sought is yours to receive."

"I'll see you around, Father."

"Definitely. Either in this world or the next, Alex."

I stood and turned, walking towards the cell door while the guard opened and closed the heavy steel door behind me. Alex made no movements. Perfectly still. Staring. His silence rang through my head as loud as his stories. I knew we would meet again but wasn't sure if the circumstances would be the same. His soul was so tortured on Earth that even Hell wouldn't faze him.

\#

CHAPTER NINE

"And you shall be to me a kingdom of priests and a holy nation." Exodus 19:6

Following the discussion I had with Alex at the prison, I became more interested in his case. I searched through old news articles that included details that pertained to not only his crimes, but his eventual arrest. Surely, there would be a place in Heaven for such a damned soul on Earth? He had done what anyone would do in that scenario. I began to feel as though the attacks were justified. Alex was only ridding the world of those awful sinners, but justice was skewed. These thoughts bothered me for the ensuing weeks, all the way up until graduation in the spring.

I managed to complete my time at the St. John's Seminary and was assigned a position with Father Shaun at St. Christopher's Parish as an additional priest. I was given several roles, including mass services in the middle of the week, as well as ensuring the holy water was filled after service confessionals. Father Shaun would continue to lead the Saturday and Sunday masses, as he had the tenure and guidance for those that were regular members of the congregation.

"Thomas, congratulations! We are so glad to have you here! You are the piece of our puzzle that has been missing!" Father Shaun said with a massive enthusiasm.

"Thank you, Father Shaun. It feels great to be back home with everyone. Especially since my grandmother's health is not the greatest. Have you had a chance to visit her lately?"

"Every day. I make it a point to have coffee with her, ever since your grandfather passed. You know, she was worried about you at one point? But look how far you've come! We're so excited to have you back here!" Father Shaun exclaimed as he wrapped his arm around my shoulder, and we proceeded into the parish center next door for lunch.

The weeks that followed were mundane. Services. Confessionals. Last Rites. All the things that the seminary had prepared me for. I would meet and greet every single member of the congregation during this time, learning who they were and what their lives were like.

There was Margie Balfort, a devout Catholic her whole life, who had spent time serving as the parish administrator in the seventies. She had retired some years ago and now made it a point to be at every service. Her young face would lead some to believe she was in her early sixties, but her soft-spoken demeanor let you know that she was much older. Her husband had passed and now she spent her free time knitting and playing cards at the local Knights of Columbus branch.

Charlie Whipper was a mid-twenty-something cook at a local diner. He was boisterous about his life outside of the church, but his parents had made certain to raise him in the church, including sending him to St. Christopher's Private School across the road. Occasionally, he would show up with his apron still thrown over his shoulder, as his overnight shift ended right before mass began.

Another regular of the services was Janet Clemont. Always dressed in the nicest attire, she made sure that she was seen by the rest of the congregation. Her head held high, she had acquired a large inheritance from her family's butcher shop. Her hands would let you know that she had never cut a single piece of meat in her life. Though she carried herself in the highest of regard, the offering plate would pass her hands empty.

The church was full of an assortment of individuals from different backgrounds. All of them had one thing in common though: their commitment to our church. I would occasionally serve them penance in the confessionals, and other times I would bless their dying family members. The services we offered to them gave their faith, the light in the darkest of times. I was proud to serve them all.

#

CHAPTER TEN

"If we confess our sins, he is faithful and just to forgive us our sins..." 1 John 1:9

I can recall the very moment that the normality of my post-seminary life would cease to be. I had finished a service one Wednesday afternoon and had scheduled open confessionals for the evening. The church appeared to have cleared out and I had thanked the remaining members as they filed out the large, wooden church doors. As usual, I had decided to proceed to the confessional booth as it was customary for a few members to return in search of penance. I sat down inside the small, dimly lit booth and had just opened my Bible for some reading.

"Hello, Father," a voice sounded out from the adjacent booth.

I was startled as I had not heard the door open and close. "Hello?"

"My apologies, Father. I didn't mean to frighten you."

"It's fine. What ails you?"

"Nothing, Father."

"What can I help you with then?"

"You remember us, Father?"

"I'm sorry I don't follow..." I questioned, making sure to continue looking forward into the light slightly beaming through the crack of the door.

"We used to visit you, Thomas. We were with you in the most trying of times."

I sat motionless as my heart began to flutter. I could feel my pulse start to move through the veins in my neck.

"Surely you remember us? We were there when your mother and your grandfather passed, Thomas."

My heart sank deep into my chest as I struggled to push the air through my lungs. My tongue felt paralyzed against the bottom of my mouth, unable to speak a single word. The stagnant air evaporated all saliva from the lining of my throat.

"Don't be afraid, Father. We won't hurt you. We need you. You need us. We are the gateway to your salvation. Your calling is through us. God demands it."

The sweat began to trickle from my forehead and onto the holiest of books situated on my lap.

"Father. Their sins. The seven. Return them to us. Bring them to their eternal damnation. God wills it. You must deliver. Their end is nigh. Bring them to us!" the voice in the darkness screamed out as I bolted through the confessional doors.

Running through the empty church, I hurried to the doors, flinging them open as I made my way down to the front of the cathedral. My blood pressure pushing a red flush onto my face and the drenched garments of the robe sticking to my skin. Eyes the size of small saucers, I knelt down and began to pray. A prayer of guidance. A prayer for safety. The prayer for eternal forgiveness.

#

CHAPTER ELEVEN

"...without the shedding of blood there is no forgiveness of sins." Hebrews 9:22

My mind was spinning circles for the next few days. Focus during mass was nearly impossible as I combed through my own sermons looking for a guiding passage, but the pages felt blank. The feeling of confusion and anxiousness was compounded by the unrelenting amount of tasks I had been given. I would walk aimlessly down hospital hallways on my way to perform last rites for a dying faithful, only to occasionally catch a shadow standing to the side of an open doorway.

The prayers for those in their final moments were even more cruel to my spirit, as I would stare into the pages of the holiest of books and recite the passages without emotion. My consciousness was fixated on the discussion in the confessional. That screeching voice echoed through my mind like a church choir that would not be silenced, choosing to sing over any prayers that were uttered.

I eventually decided to refer to Father Shaun about the incident. His recommendation was to take a few more days away from my service to the church, but I assured him that the church would only serve to strengthen my mind, and hesitantly, he agreed. I did not give immediate details, only referring to the voice as an almost threatening tone. He sounded almost certain that it was a prank. This was the succor that was very much needed.

Over the course of the following days, I felt unsettled. It was the feeling of being watched. My peripheral was constantly haunted by shadows inside the cathedral as the sun would shift throughout the day. No matter how hard I would try to draw my attention elsewhere or shake it off, my nervous scanning of the room as constant. Luckily, I was to pay another visit to the local prison for services and confessional. Never had a place with such depressing decor been such a welcome sight.

I arrived as usual and checked in with the guards, when I was stopped by the warden on my way to the prison's chaplain quarters.

"Good afternoon, Father. I have had a request for you. It's an interesting one."

"Oh? How so?"

"It appears you've got a pal? The Handyman, Alex Fulmer, wants to speak with you. He's got some confessions he wants to make." The warden seemed interested, as his stare, coupled with the flex of his eyebrows, informed me.

"Sure. I can meet with him today after mass. No problem."

"Listen Father, can you do us a favor?"

"That depends on the favor, but I will definitely try to accommodate. What can I help you with?"

"We've been trying to get some info about those murders he committed. If you wouldn't mind passing any certain details along, it would be appreciated."

"Unfortunately, Warden, I'm bound to an oath that's higher than any judge or jury on Earth. Anything I hear in that cell, once it enters my ears, cannot leave my mouth. That is, unless you're above an oath to our savior, Jesus Christ?"

The warden understood, but the angry look of disappointment on his face meant that he was not pleased with my answer. This was all fine to me as I had committed myself to serving a being that was higher than even the warden. The guards opened the doors and into the den of despair I was led.

When we reached Alex's cell, he was positioned exactly how I had previously left him. A body that lacked the driving motor of a soul. However, when the cell door shut behind me, he came back to life, as if he was on a commercial break from some episodic television show he had watched in his youth. I sat down next to him as he began to wet his lips and shifted his head towards the floor.

"It's good to see you again, Father."

"Likewise, Alex. How have things been going with you?" I said looking around the room and noticing a well-placed Holy Bible sitting on a small, stainless steel shelf near his bedside. "Reading the good word?"

"No. That came from the Old Bastard's personal collection. His favorite coaster. Don't recall it serving any other purpose."

"I understand. Do you ever think that if he had maybe opened it that your situation would be different?"

"Nah. The feeling to get rid of those creatures would still be there. Maybe they were there before he did what he did." Alex gritted his teeth, staring blankly at the cold cement wall in front of him.

"Like a calling?" I nervously questioned.

"Yeah, like a calling. Maybe the Old Bastard was the catalyst to wake me up."

I sat silent for a moment, watching the hamster begin to turn on the wheel inside of Alex's head, his eyes reading across the wall as if he was looking for answers to questions I couldn't hear. After about a minute or two of waiting patiently for his eyes to fixate in a central location, I decided it was safe to continue the conversation. I had been warned by the prison guards to mind his mannerisms and to be aware of his mood shifts, especially being in a vulnerable position alone in the cell.

"Do you think it was your own decision or maybe a calling higher than yourself to do what you did, Alex?"

"I don't believe in that shit. None of it. No God would let what happened to me happen. It's all a bunch of bullshit."

"Perhaps, but what if it was God's will? What if the terrible things that happened to you were God's way of moving you to get rid of the others, like..."

"Like the Old Bastard?" Alex turned and stared directly into my eyes, letting me know that the line had been drawn. "Well, if that's the case, His approach was a bit off, don't ya think? I mean, killing those assholes gave me such a relief. I haven't been with a woman, but I can imagine that's the kind of feeling I got smashing those fuckin' rats over the head. You think God made me do that, Father? Is that where you're going with this?" Alex's stone-cold glare was beaming through me now and into the wall behind.

"Maybe God wanted mercy for those that couldn't help themselves. You saved those children, Alex. There must have been something besides your own past and your urges that drove you to murder those people."

"I did what I did because I had to. Simple as that. Feeling good about it was just a bonus. If God wanted things to play out the way they did, then there should be a whole hell of a lot more people worried."

My attention was now fixated on everything that Alex had to say.

"There are worse sins than what I've done. You know this. What do you holy men call them? Seven deadliest sins?"

"The seven deadly sins."

"That's right." He chuckled as he continued on. "Aren't those the worst of the worst? The ones who get the bad side of our Lord and savior? I've seen some of them right in here. Nasty, unkempt, and greedy shits. I'm sure there are plenty outside these walls, too. I'd be willing to bet there are even a few sitting down to pray in your very pews today. Would you like to wager, Father?" The condescending tone in his voice gave way to certainty.

The room had declined to an almost freezing temperature. The silence that followed sent shivers through my body as he smiled and shook his head.

Was there something that he knew?

"Well, I think our time today is over."

"Before you go, Father, tell me one more thing. Do you ever get urges? Do you ever feel like there's a calling that you're not giving in to? Maybe something that doesn't sit right but you feel compelled to do? Like God is giving you signs?"

My body froze in that moment. A sudden sense of dread surrounded me, and I could feel an uneasy feeling creeping into my soul. I yelled for the guards, my back to the cell door, watching as Alex's demeanor shifted back into the statuesque pose. No smiles. No voice. Just looking for answers in a dull, pale gray wall.

\#

CHAPTER TWELVE

"If you forgive the sins of any, they are forgiven them; if you withhold forgiveness, it is withheld." John 20:23

Driving home from the prison, I couldn't help but reflect back on what Alex had said about the seven deadly sins, about what that creature in the confessional had requested, and the lingering urge to dig deeper. I arrived back at the parish center just in time for the evening service to begin. I watched as each individual member of the congregation waltzed into the doors, on their way to be forgiven of all the sins they had committed, while cell-block saviors like Alex sat behind bars waiting to meet the man who put them there. I felt an overwhelming sense of responsibility in the moment. The undeniable desire to give into the request that had been handed down to me from above.

The discussion in the prison festered relentlessly inside my mind the next few days. Mass would come and go, and I spent time in between prayers and incantations looking for answers. The long litany of prayers that I recited looking for direct answers yielded no results. That is, until it came time the following week to observe penance among the members of the congregation.

"Forgive me, Father, for I have sinned. It's been 130 days since my last confession," a woman behind the shifted divider spoke out.

"What is bothering you, my child of God?" I breathed out.

"I've been working so hard for our diocese and not one person has said 'thank you' or 'we appreciate you.' It's been bothering me so much, and I know it's wrong. I know we do service for the Lord, but I also believe that I deserve some respect for all that I do. I appreciate you so much, Father, but no one has noticed all the hard work I have committed. In fact, I even put a special thank-you myself in the church bulletin but was skipped over when Father Shaun read out the bullet points last week. I'm just..."

"My child, the Lord loves and respects everything you do for the witness of others. Please know that you won't always be noticed on Earth, but you will be rewarded in Heaven. Do not think that you are overlooked but rather work in silence and respect the rewards that you will reap in the face of the holiest of holies," I recited, knowing exactly who was sitting on the other side of that divider.

I felt a cold sensation overcome my body as I waited for her reply and request of forgiveness. I turned and stared into the darkness next to me where the woman's voice had come from, yet it was replaced with a voice that terrified me.

"Pride, Father. It's all she's known. She doesn't deserve to serve this congregation. Look at how petty she is. Her intentions are to be above you. She craves the attention and would love nothing more than to be done with you and your entitlements in the church. You must give her to us, Father. She commits one of the seven. You must release her. God wills it!" a screeching voice screamed out as I pushed my back to the adjacent wall of the confessional.

"Father? Are you alright over there? I'm sorry if I upset you..." the woman's voice questioned.

"No, Mar—ma'am. I...I think I saw a spider in here. I'm not too fond of them, that's all," I jokingly replied as I attempted to gain my breath back. "Ten Hail Mary's and three Lord's Prayers should be sufficient, ma'am. I will hear from you again soon." I shoved the wooden divider window shut and sat staring into the door of the booth.

I listened in as the woman slowly shuffled out of the booth and went on her way. I knew what had happened and I knew what was requested of me. I had no choice but to serve the calling of our Lord, even if that meant giving a life to the evils that had overtaken her soul. The voice was calling to me and I had to receive. I was certain that sending away those that had wronged the Lord and his servants on Earth would cleanse the sins of others. This act of penance would give guidance to those looking to potentially pursue a sin of no return. I had decided to receive my calling. A calling of eternal salvation from eternal damnation.

#

CHAPTER THIRTEEN

"Pride goes before destruction, and a haughty spirit before a fall." Proverbs 16:18

The sinking feeling in my stomach, the sweats from the nervous pulses, and the constant audible whistles of the wind, served to bring me to my knees in prayer daily. I continued to ask for a sign that there was another way. Yet, there was no answer from above. Only continued silence. Margie Belfort had served our church for so long, but her pride had grown too large to escape. The voices had called her, and my charge was to return the evil to its proper place, in Hell. Tortured for days between the reality of what was to come and the pleas for guidance eventually wore thin. Broken from the anxiety, I eventually came to terms with my responsibility.

Margie kept a regular schedule. She would wake and slumber at the same exact time every day. Her routine made it easy to find the perfect time to proceed with the act of absolution. I watched through

Margie's open windows from my old, blue 1970s pickup that I had received as inheritance from my grandfather. It was quiet and served to keep my visibility to a minimum. Margie would return from her daily tasks of visiting the local cafe with her friends for coffee, going to the church for prayer, having lunch, and visiting the salon.

She was extremely proud of how well-kept she was. Her hair and nails were properly manicured, her jewelry always clean and clothes unwrinkled. The more I observed, the more I understood why she had been called. The pride had blinded her to the humility that was preached so often in my sermons. The message had become lost in her selfishness, and there was no time left to reiterate.

Her house was just as haughty as I had expected. The fine china cabinet in the dining room with not an ounce of dust, the rug that had not a single string straggling from it, the flower vase on the dining room table, and the smell of mothballs emanating from the closet in the hallway. It was that closet that I chose to climb into and wait. When Margie arrived back at her home, I peered through the cracked door as she went about her business preparing for bed. The very bed that would be the last place she slept.

You are doing right by the Lord, Thomas. Don't forget why you were brought here. This is what needs to happen.

I patiently waited till Margie turned her lamp off and quickly fell into a deep sleep. I had remembered the discussions with Alex in the prison and how he had avoided capture by leaving the scene immediately after the crime. At this moment, I was able to recall the entire story of each creature he had sent back to Hell. I was to do a similar bidding to appease the angels who had sent me here. Placing a pair of black latex gloves on my hands and pulling my mask down, I slowly crept towards the dormant Margie Belfort, then quietly pulled the window shut that was propped open next to her bed. I hesitated.

What if she wakes up? What if it takes several goes at her to revoke her time on Earth?

I pulled the knife out from my belt and grabbed for the pillow that sat beside Mrs. Belfort. She started to wake and reach for her glasses.

"Hello? Is...is someone there?"

I could feel the sweat start to drench the black cotton mask as my breathing began to increase. The flow of blood through my restricted veins felt like the fires of Hell rushing to escape my body, but there was no exit, only a heatwave of pressure. Shoving the pillow into her face as her glasses met her opening eyes, I drew the knife back with my other hand, repeatedly bringing the blade through the soft pillow and into the fleshy bone underneath it. She screamed. She screamed a horrid scream while the blood began to soak through the compressed down pillow. Up and down. Up and down. My eyes closed as the sharpened blade of the knife fell into her until there was no motion or audible sounds. I pulled the knife back and fell against the closet doors beside the sleigh bed that contained the remnants of a prideful sinner.

I quickly fled from the house through the back door, jumping into my truck and driving as fast as possible. I drove with my eyes fixated on the road like a junkie high from their first fix. adrenaline pushing rhythmically through my body as the drum beat of my heart continued to pound. I couldn't remember how long I drove or where I drove to, but when I came to, I was standing in the shower, the blood trickling into the drain as an immense dread poured into my head, nearly stopping my heart.

What have I done? Is it over? Are they happy now? Is God happy? Did anyone notice me?

The bed brought no comfort. No relief. I stared at the ceiling the entirety of the night while replaying the events over and over again. I could hear the muffled screams reverberate throughout the walls of my room, or maybe it was my mind. The sound of the knife tugging through flesh, grinding across bone, and the squishing of facial and internal features played like a soundtrack to a 70s horror film. There was no film though, only a grim reality of what I had been summoned to do. Eventually, the exhaustion came for me as my eyes permitted me to sleep against my mind's wishes. There would be no more sleep though, only death and forgiveness.

#

CHAPTER FOURTEEN

"But each person is tempted when he is lured and enticed by his own desire." James 1:14

Guilt could be such a heavy burden. It seeped into the very folds of the mind that were reserved for the happy memories. It ran an endless loop that passed through stages such as grief, angst, and self-hatred. I tried to escape it for the next few days and eventually, my physical appearance drew questions from the members of the congregation and Father Shaun. He managed to corner me one afternoon following the midday service.

"Thomas, you alright? You look like you might be a little tired?"

"I'm fine, just getting over a touch of the flu. It's been plaguing me since last week and it hit me hard the past few days. I'll make it." The lie snuck through my teeth as the look on Father Shaun's face grew into deeper concern.

"Why don't you take tomorrow off? Maybe get some rest and then we'll see how you feel on Thursday?"

"Sure. I appreciate that."

The day off was welcome but I knew what was to occupy my time. There were not enough verses in the Holy Bible to make me forget what I had done. I prayed and prayed in my room, asking for forgiveness. Conflicted by the very thought of my savior asking me to commit such an atrocity but also understanding that God's will was not always clear to me.

Maybe the voices and the figures I had seen were simply the essence of God in a form I could not comprehend?

After hours had passed sitting in my recliner, Bible in hand, I began to catch swift movements from across the room. Silent shadows passing across the walls just outside of my full field of vision.

"You did good, Father. Don't blame yourself for the sins of others, for that is the millstone our Lord carries for you. He is pleased with your servitude. Please Him again, and the rewards will be reaped for eternity." My skin crawled at the sound of the voice reverberating throughout my mind.

Startled, I stood up and began to look in every direction in the room, but there was nothing. No person, no dark being, and no semblance of a human. After inspecting the rest of the house, I noticed that my King James Bible had fallen from the recliner to the floor. The book lay wide open, and, upon inspection, I noticed a verse I had previously highlighted.

Many are the plans in the mind of a man, but it is the purpose of the Lord that will stand.

Proverbs 19:21

The words and their meaning broke through mind like a light shining through a damp and dark fogginess. These tasks that were given to me were not for me to question; rather, I was to put all my trust in the requests of the Lord. These were simply trials of vindication of my faith. In that moment, I had finally received the peace that these killings had meaning. They weren't simply random members of the congregation being led to the slaughter by a trick of the devil. These were slights against the Lord.

The convictions of these deviant monsters were meant to persuade others to follow their path. My actions had meaning. My own mother had aggrieved God for all the terrible things that had happened to her. Her sin, gluttony, had strangled her veins and sent her to dine alongside the other unwelcomed. I could feel the resentment build as I realized her decision to continue to use was a sin that was not forgiven.

She was the catalyst for this. She was no martyr for me. God's will had always been to lead me here. Lead me to punish the wicked. My own mother, an unwelcomed in the eyes of our Lord. *She will dine on toads and burn for her sins, I am certain.*

Confronting the will of God brought me comfort. It allowed me to come to terms with everything that had happened. It brought me peace. The peace you found when you understood that there was no end to this game of life. Just a second verse that a select few got the opportunity to read.

#

CHAPTER FIFTEEN

"Create in me a clean heart, O God, and renew a right spirit within me." Psalm 51:10

Days and nights passed with regular rotation. I found myself wondering when the next calling would be or if they would return. Confessionals were scheduled in the next few days, and I realized that I was to deliver another unwelcomed being to their judgement. I spent the following days gazing at the potential members who would be interested in passing through that booth.

"Father Abner, your sermon today was fantastic. It really spoke to me on all levels. You know you could have been a motivational speaker?" Mrs. Clemont boasted as she twirled her pearl necklace that reflected the light from the open church doors.

"You know, Janet, I thought about it sometime before I found my calling. I'm sure it pays well, here on Earth. Probably much better than a priest. But I wouldn't be able to assist those dealing with greed.

Say, I'm not trying to be rude, but a few of the other parishioners mentioned that you passed on the offering plate. Everything alright, financially?"

"Oh, Father, you know that I give my time to the church in exchange for monetary offerings. If I gave money at every service, then there wouldn't be any left for me to take care of my parents with. You know how it is, right?"

I grit my teeth and smiled. The Clemont family was wealthy from an oil field that had sat on their property in Texas for the past sixty years. Janet Clemont's parents had always given an offering to the church, until they were introduced into a nursing home by their daughter and became unable to attend service. Her parents had spent much of her youth spoiling her with money as dark as the oil beneath their feet.

"I understand. I did want to know if you saw that we're granting penance later this week? You know that it not only clears your mind but your spirit as well!" I said with a smile that stretched across my face.

"I know, Father, and I promise I will make it back in eventually. Although, I don't have too much bother right now. Being busy with my parents is like a full-time job, ya know?"

"Yes. Yes, of course. I'll pray for you anyway. How's that sound?"

"Thank you, Father Thomas. We are truly blessed to have you here with us."

I watched as she descended the stairs in front of the church and waltzed to her new sports car. My eyes fixated on the transgressor as she pulled from the curb of the St. Christopher's Cathedral. I had begun to walk back inside towards the sacristy when I was approached by Father Shaun and an unknown individual.

"Father Thomas, this Detective Matthew Gilmour, he's from the 11th District Precinct."

The objects in the room began to get blurry as if I had started to spin. The air deflated from my body as I stood in shock. I could feel my heart began to play hymns of horror.

"Afternoon, Father," he said as his dry palm met the sweat that had begun to pour from mine. "Sorry to bother you. I'm investigating a possible murder of one of your churchgoers. Are you familiar with a Margie Belfort by chance?"

"Margie? Yea...Yes, I am. Why what's going on? You said murder?"

"Unfortunately, we found Margie deceased yesterday. She didn't show up to the salon for a few days and I guess the ladies in the shop started to get worried. We went over and checked on her, and it was pretty grisly, to be honest. Do you know if she had anyone that was upset with her?"

I swallowed every last drop of saliva in my mouth as I searched for a response in my head. "No, no. Everyone loved Margie here. She's been with the church for years longer than I have. I've never heard anyone say a sour thing about that wonderful woman."

"Father Shaun said the exact same thing," Detective Gilmour said as he made notes in his black notebook. "Listen, if either of you catch wind of someone talking about anything suspicious, don't hesitate to call. Whoever did this really didn't care much for that lady. Made Swiss cheese out of her. You have my card. And hey, that's a nice necklace you got. My grandad used to wear one just like it."

"It was a gift from a long time ago. It's the emblem of St. Christopher."

"Yeah, yeah, sure. Keep us posted, would ya?"

Father Shaun stood holding his mouth as Detective Gilmour wandered down the aisle and back out of the church doors. "Thomas, please keep your eyes and ears open. I'm concerned for anyone else that might run into this crazy person."

"I will, Father," I assured him.

The relief hit me like a breath of air after nearly being suffocated. I bent down into the pew and sat. The sinking feeling in my stomach had returned and the guilt brought me to the ledge under the pew, where I knelt and began to pray. I prayed that I was doing right by the Lord, and all would come to be forgiven, for all.

Against my better judgement, I made the decision to visit a local liquor store and pick up a bottle of whiskey. The young man behind the counter cracked jokes about a priest coming to buy a single pint of top-shelf whiskey. His witty humor and careless demeanor served to calm my uncomfortable nerves. Leaving the store, I noticed a rough-looking individual sitting in his car next to my truck, a hard hat and leather gloves resting together on the dashboard. He smiled and laughed to himself as he climbed out of the vehicle.

"Hey, Father, rough night?" the man said as he started towards the storefront doorway.

I stopped dead in my tracks.

"You could say that."

"Care for a confession?" he laughed and waited for me to reply.

"Nope, nothing to confess here. What about yourself?"

"Father, I have about fifteen different confessions to make, but they aren't for you," he said jokingly as he continued inside.

I slammed the door, clinched the steering wheel tightly, and sat staring through the windshield. I could sense the jitteriness of my body as it shook from the trepidation of being caught. The small pint of liquor did little to suppress my anxiousness and guilt. I sped towards my home with hopes that I wouldn't be pulled over as I took small sips from the bottle, finishing it as I pulled into the driveway. I stumbled inside, catching myself in my recliner as the room began to spin. Watching the large box television morph shapes as I struggled to maintain my mental capabilities, I noticed it standing near a window.

The being that had been following me. I hadn't mentioned it to anyone, but I had seen it over the course of the days that had followed Margie's descent. The stare was hypnotic, almost trance-like. I found myself staring into the blank nothingness that covered my entire vision. Then, there was nothing. Startled, I looked everywhere around the room, bringing my eyes to rest on the large television in front of me. A slender, dark arm reached out from the static of the screen and beckoned me towards it.

The arm continued inward till it disappeared into the bright, glitchy background of the static. Suddenly, the television shifted from distorted lines to the local newscast. Two newscasters, seated, with a picture of Margie Belfort situated to the top right of the screen.

"And now, for tonight's main story. Police have confirmed they have had no leads in the homicide of local church elder, Margie Belfort. Detectives are urging anyone with information to please call into the Chicago Police Department Tip Line. You never know when your information could help police solve a terrible crime."

I sat back as the tension fled from my body. The worries of the day had disintegrated into a pile of misplaced feelings. Internally, there were celebrations of relief that could have lit the darkest of skies with multicolored lights. Mental fireworks of comfort.

#

CHAPTER SIXTEEN

"No, I tell you; but unless you repent, you will all likewise perish." Luke 13:3

Feelings are a funny thing. One minute you could be fine, stressed the next, and then be on top of the world. God had shown me that he would protect me and the news presentation the evening before was all the validation that I needed. I was now, more than ever, prepared to continue to serve, the very reason I had been led through the shadows of a terrible existence and into the church. I had been called to serve death to those that felt they were above the laws of Heaven. These deviant preternatural fiends of sin that walked this earth had to be brought to the ultimate justice.

Days slipped into weeks as I continued watching members of the congregation detour from the path that God had put them on. I eventually landed on the next individual who would come to know the fear of the most holy. The corrupted individual was Charlie Whipper.

He worked at a local restaurant, which was owned by one of the other members of our congregation. He worked the closing shift and maintained the evening deposits for the eatery.

He had been notorious in his early youth for being a thief that wouldn't even pay the shop owners the respect of looking around before he threw something into his pockets. His fearlessness led him to stand before a judge and even be sent to a reformatory for troubled youth. Upon release, his transgressions had been forgotten by the community, but even after a lengthy stint in a cell, his old habits had died hard.

"Father, please forgive me. It's been a while since I've stopped in here and I need to get something off my chest, if ya don't mind?"

"Surely, my son. What is bothering you so much this afternoon?"

"Well, Father, I've felt like I've been getting screwed...er...shafted at work. I spend all my time taking care of the business I work at and Mitch...I...mean, the boss isn't giving me the respect I deserve. I'm making him all this money in the evenings and he's just pocketing it all. It's a bunch of...bologna, Father. I decided that it's time I get my fair share and went ahead and pocketed some of the money from a few evening regulars' bills. I figured that he'll never know since I take care of everything. I think I'm owed that, Father. Do you agree?"

I had hit the unholy lottery. A two-for-one special. Charlie was filled with both greed and envy. Two separate sins that would call for extra attention when dealing with them. The heavenly father above was going to be most pleased, and I couldn't wait to appease Him as I continued on the righteous path.

"My son, please refrain from continuing these actions and take care in knowing that our lord and savior will grant you all the riches of heaven upon entry. I would suggest giving an extra offering in penance, as well as providing the Lord with several prayers in exchange for the forgiveness he will offer you."

"Thanks, Father. I appreciate it. I'll take care of that this week."

I listened as Charlie left the confessional booth and out the heavy doors of the cathedral. The smell of fried food lingering on his clothes was a dead giveaway of his previous evening's work. The rich smell of grease had followed him at every encounter we had previously had and let me know exactly who was to meet with their judge later this week.

The following evenings were spent surveilling Charlie as he went about his business inside of the restaurant. He was consistent with his arrival and departure from the diner, carrying the deposit bag down Main Street to the nearby bank and dropping it into the depository. Every evening, he would reach his hand into the bag to grab a small handful of cash and place it into his pocket as he walked down the street to the bank. Surely, he was doing this to prevent being seen by any of his coworkers who would occasionally stick behind to help Charlie clean up.

I made the decision to wait one evening as he dropped off the deposit bag and headed to his car. Stepping in near unison, I approached him with a slow stride watching as a dark figure ahead of us pointed and smiled. They were watching to make sure I completed the exercise I had been requested to. I knew it was them because their teeth shined white, as you would expect an angel's teeth to shine. Charlie continued to walk in the direction of his car, spinning his keys on his finger and humming a tune that I was not familiar with.

The keys dropped from his finger, stopping us both in our tracks. When he bent over to grab the keys, I made my move towards him. Chloroform-laced rag in hand, I grabbed around his mouth. He bit down and began a very short struggle that eventually led him to the ground in an unconscious state.

After pulling the car up and dragging his body towards the truck bed, I lifted him inside and slammed the lid close. I grabbed an old rug, throwing it on top, and also placed a blue painter's tarp on top to obstruct any view. No one was around. The truck pulled from the curb, and I headed towards an old, dilapidated and abandoned home that was across town from mine. I had passed it many times enroute to the prison and decided it would serve as a ritual site for the next transgressor.

Blue and red lights suddenly flashed across the inside of my truck as I moved towards the shoulder, expecting the lights to pass, yet they did not. The receding sweat began to pour again as I watched and waited for the officer's flashlight to move towards the front of the truck.

"Evening. What's the rush, Father?" the officer questioned as he peered around the outskirts of the truck bed.

"Oh, well..." I scrambled to find a reason and not draw suspicion. "I'm going to clean some rugs before tomorrow's service. I got busy and forgot to take care of it earlier. The members have a tendency to leave more than their sins at the door, Officer."

"I see..." He began to open the tarp.

I shout from the front, "You know, Officer?"

He turned and glanced back over to the front of the truck cab, shining his light inside, blinding me completely. "What?"

"Cleanliness is next to godliness. We can't have the House of God looking like a mud pile, now, can we?"

"Guess not. Try and slow it down a bit. We don't need you rushing off to Heaven on us, Father."

I watched through the rearview mirror as the officer settled into his cruiser and slowly drove past with a continued look of skepticism. The air in my lungs blasted outward through my throat and into the cabin. I felt the lump in my throat return back into the fiery pit of my stomach. The exchange brought me to a realization that even though I was protected by the Holy Spirit, I still needed to carry my senses. I shifted the old truck into drive and continued onwards to the vacant property.

#

CHAPTER SEVENTEEN

"For it is impossible for the blood of bulls and goats to take away sins." Hebrews 10:4

Charlie's dead weight was difficult to drag into the building, but I managed to drag him just inside the door, enough to pull it shut and lock the deadbolt. The house was in a mostly deserted part of the city that had been lost to the exodus of manufacturing jobs and the sharp rise in the poverty line. Though the windows were shut, I was certain that there would be limited screaming.

I managed to sit Charlie in an old vintage kitchen chair and began to tie his ankles to each of the legs of the seat. After which, I bound his mouth with a gag and began to tie his hands to the rungs behind him. Each knot was bound several times to prevent too much hassle. The black mask I wore began to itch, causing me to pause to adjust it and relieve myself of the itchiness.

They say the Lord works in mysterious ways, and on this occasion, I was to find out the truth of that cliché. While adjusting my mask, I felt it pulled from my head. My eyes were staring at the bulging baby blues of Charlie Whipper, holding the mask in hand, sweat rolling down off his forehead. At that second, the hands of every clock in the world froze.

I started to stand as Charlie gripped my leg with his untethered hand. I fell to the ground hard. Hard enough to make me nearly see stars. I shook my head to knock the night sky from my sight, catching glimpses of Charlie working to untie himself.

Charlie caught me off guard once again as I stood up, tackling me back to the ground. I quickly reached for the knife from my waistband and drew it towards Charlie as we struggled for dominance over the blade. Pushing the dagger upwards towards Charlie, his force working against mine to keep my arm subdued was like a death ritual. A promise of demise for one individual involved and the opportunity to meet his maker.

I pushed as hard as I could upwards, bringing the point of the blade mere inches from his face, and as he saw the encroaching metal shiv move upwards, he thrust his weight downward. A miracle of timing occurred as I relented and let the handle of the blade fall to the ground, causing Charlie to fall onto the knife with the full, extensive weight of his body.

He sat up. The gurgling of blood quickly gave way to a shower that covered me and the floor under Charlie. His empty gaze felt like being pierced through every inch of my being. A search for answers without a word being spoken. Every pulse brought more blood from the now gaping hole in his neck. The struggle to live, the plea for answers, and the very notion that his deeds would be punished afterwards kept him around for a few moments. He tried standing but the loss of blood prevented him from reaching his feet. He grabbed out for me but was met with my feet kicking him away in disgust and horror.

A brief attempt to continue seeing the world from this side of the void was futile. Charlie fell forward onto the old wooden planks of the house, splashing into his own blood. I couldn't move. The blood on my hands and face was a new concept. I quickly grabbed the knife, my mask, and ran for the pickup truck. When I stepped inside, the rearview mirror told a story that would mortify others. My mind was struggling to find words to pray as I took the exit that would lead to my home.

I ran upstairs, straight into the bathroom, turning on the cold water, and I sat. I sat staring. I wasn't sure what I was feeling. The whole situation was surreal. The brutality of the whole ordeal was different than Margie Belfort's relief. I didn't have to see her. I didn't have to wash copious amounts of her blood from my body. There were questions pertaining to the act that I was hoping to find answers for.

Did they accept him? I must be credited with returning him to the depths he had been birthed from, right? Surely, they will accept him as the payment due.

A sense of despair began to sink in as I clutched the emblem of St. Christopher that was bound to my neck. I had continued to wear the sign of the saint to ward off any unholy beings and to protect me from all the sinners that surrounded me. The emblem of St. Christopher was ages old, but the blood washed from it was fresh. I could feel my stomach slowly shift in my abdomen. The guilt dripped from my throat into the dark pit inside me. A chamber of awful bleakness that was slowly creeping into my mind, unable to be tamed by prayer or penance.

My mental status eroded, I decided to take long pulls from one of the wine bottles I had brought home from the church holding. I was halfway through the bottle when I could feel the disquietude bleed over into paranoia.

"You did good, Father. They were sinners of the worst variety. Your sins will be absolved. Your eternal peace is nearing. Give them to us. The harvest is ripe. Your father demands it!"

Their voices had previously never changed, but now they were tormenting me by using a voice of the earthly unwelcomed. They were preaching to me through the sound of Charlie's voice. All through the evening hours. The lack of sleep, coupled with the intense misery of visuals of blood-soaked and disfigured faces was starting to eat at me. I paced the small area inside my room until it became too much. I slumped against the wall, hands folded in prayer and slipped into a deep sleep.

By the time I woke up, I had overslept and the beeping from my answering machine let me know that there were those that were possibly worried. I quickly rushed to the phone, dialing the church secretary.

"I must apologize, I've not felt well. I believe I've come down with something, Sadie. I'll try to make it in tomorrow. I should be better by then."

"Father Abner? You weren't scheduled for mass today. Are you sure you are alright? Anything we can help you with?"

"No, Sadie. I promise everything is fine. It's just some stomach bug that has been bothering me lately."

"Well, if you need anything, please don't hesitate to call one of us. You know we will do whatever we can to help. You will be in our prayers." The concern in Sadie's voice was strong.

"Thank you. I appreciate that. I'll see you tomorrow."

"There is one more thing, Father. That police detective was back this morning asking some of the congregation questions. Said he would like to speak with you again soon, if at all possible. I told him I would relay the message."

"Th...Thanks, Sadie. I'll give him a call shortly."

The phone rested slowly back on its receiver. The world began to spin, and my eyes were drawn slowly in an empty stare. I climbed back in bed, gutted from the possibility of being caught. I spent the rest of the day staring into the ceiling, trying to fight off the anxiety with prayer. No use. Evening drew closer and the creeping sense of remorse started to draw in deeper. I opened myself to the Lord's scripture.

"For if you live according to the flesh, you will die, but if by the spirit you put to death the deeds of the body, you will live."

Romans 8:13

No physical pain could entirely dismember the torture of the soul, but perhaps it would alleviate the scourge of guilt raining down on me. I was prepared to suffer for the will of God. Any suffering would do.

#

CHAPTER EIGHTEEN

"He must increase, but I must decrease." John 3:30

The moments between finding the nearly rusted pair of pliers from the toolbox in the basement and the harsh reality that I suffered after were a blur. A vague moment of peace before the immense onslaught of self-flagellation was to begin. I had to give to be let go. I had to leave to be let in. This was His will. This was the way.

The preparation for the exercise in humility was simple. A clean towel was placed just under where my right foot would eventually rest. Dipping my foot into a brine of salt water, I let it soak to alleviate any potential for infection to take me early and to aid in the limberness that might be needed. The hand towel I had carried into the room was smashed between my teeth to keep them from breaking under the pressure of the pain.

They were watching. I could sense it. The hallway was filled with empty figures, eager for the relief of my sins. I had a duty that I was now committed to. The very fact that I felt guilt meant that I was not trusting in the Lord and his way. I had been treading on a sin that was equal to the others who had paid for their acts with their soul. They were to be damned to a fiery eternity filled with the most awful of beings. I refused to join them. I knew that hell would welcome all, but I was not to be detoured there.

I grabbed the pliers in my hand, gripping the handles with a wobble and placing the metal prongs against my salt-soaked foot. The metal of the pliers gripped around my toe, the towel snug between my teeth. I began to ask for forgiveness and requested that all my prayers be heard with the intention of receiving the penance that others were refused. A quick twist from the pliers purged my pinkie toe from its home.

I gripped the towel tight, screaming through the cloth in agony. Blood began to pour from the gaping wound, spilling onto the towel and quickly soaking in with a red stain. The salt burned as I reached for another towel to wrap it in. Pulsating pain continued up my leg. The bone fragment exposed, I continued to pray for the mercy of Heaven to be shown.

Downing a sip of the whiskey I had stored away, I cried, not in agony, but in hopes that all was forgiven. Hopes that the pain I was experiencing was enough for the Lord to hear my pleas and pardon me. I began to bandage the throbbing wound and continued to search the bottom of the whiskey bottle for the end of the suffering. After almost an hour, I was able to drag myself to my bed, passing out as the blood continued to bleed through the gauze wrapped multiple times around my foot.

Lord, please grant me access to your mercy and allow me to enter your kingdom when my time on Earth has ended. I beg you.

\#

CHAPTER NINETEEN

"Flee from sexual immorality." 1 Corinthians 6:18

Several hours later, I awoke to the sun peering through my windows and casting itself across my face. The pain of earlier coupled with the hangover of the alcohol urged me to drag myself to the bathroom. A trail of blood from the saturated medical gauze following behind, I reached the toilet. Vomiting from the malaise of the evening's events, I coated the bowl and hung my head down. Surely, the dues had been paid.

I slowly grabbed the walls as I stood myself up, tearing my clothes from my body and lying prone in the shower as the steam filled the room. The drain continuously drank the blood as I tended to the now uncovered area where my small toe had once been. I managed to stand against the wall, fighting the spins and inhaling the steam as it rose from the floor of the shower. I could smell the iron from the blood as it evaporated in the heat.

After an hour of working to regain my wits, I stumbled out and began to prep myself for the day. The superficial injuries from last night's struggle and the loss of balance made dressing myself a significant problem, but I powered onward. I scrubbed my teeth till my gums bled, trying to rid myself of the alcohol odor that had lodged itself in my throat. I questioned whether service was needed that day, but there were still sinners out there. Still more of them that needed to be released.

The sermon was short. The benediction, forgotten. I managed to push through as the congregation looked on confused. It was noticeable to everyone that something was wrong.

"Thomas, are you alright? You look pale. Maybe that flu is still present?" Father Shaun asked as he placed his hand on my shoulder post-service.

"Yeah, I think it's still there. I should probably make my way back and lie down for a bit."

"That's probably a good idea. Also, that detective was in again, asking the parishioners questions. He's going to find who did that to Margie. Don't let yourself get sicker by worrying about that. She's surely in the Lord's hands now."

I could feel my face turn flush. "I'm gonna go ahead back now and lie down. Thank you, Father." I turned and attempted to retreat as quickly as possible.

As I was hobbling down the stairs, an all too familiar voice rang out. "Father Thomas! Did you do something to your leg?"

It was Janet Clemont.

"It's just a sprain, Janet. I promise, I'll be fine."

"Oh, Father, you have to be careful. We need you to be in top form every week. How else am I going to receive penance?" She smirked as she walked away.

I shrugged it off as I had no intent on trying to convince her to attend. Furthermore, I couldn't remember her ever once attending confessional. It was not like her, but the fact that someone as full of themselves would notice my limp drew concern. The rest of the afternoon was spent working on keeping a steady walking pace while still struggling through the pain that extended up towards my knee.

The will of the Lord could not be compromised. I decided to take a couple days to reset, clear my head and allow the wound to heal. Carrying on as normal, the church members were none the wiser and I was quickly able to occupy my time with the doldrum tasks of the week. That is, until it came time for the sacrament of penance. This confessional wasn't from the booth, but rather a seedy bar near my home that I had been frequenting. It was your run-of-the-mill dive bar, complete with any sinner you could imagine.

I would routinely order an old-fashioned, place it on the back cover of my Bible, and let my mind wonder. There was something to being surrounded by the lost souls that would drown their sins in whiskey tumblers that made me feel at peace. These were heathens that had no problem with showing their true selves. It was akin to a shark swimming in a blood-tainted pool of dying fish. Their ends pending the threshold of my appetite.

"What's a man of God doing in a place like this?" a scantily clothed younger woman whispered as she sat on the barstool beside me.

"Praying."

"Praying, huh? Sure, there ain't other places you can do that?" She was persistent.

"There are, but I prefer the company of others late in the evening."

She wrapped the gum from her mouth around her finger and continued to twirl it in circles as she chewed loudly. "Oh, I guess that makes sense. I imagine it's pretty lonely being a man of God, huh?"

She scanned me up and down as I continued to stare into the mirror behind the bar.

"It can be, but that's why I'm here."

"So, what do they call you? Just Father? You got a name behind that, Father?"

"Father Thomas. Just Father Thomas."

We sat quietly for a few moments. My nerves were slightly elevated, due to the combination of stress and alcohol. I had never run into this woman any other night I had wandered in looking for a drink or an opportunity to witness. Looking into the mirror, I could see the reflection of the darkened bathroom hallway behind us. A slender black arm began stretching out from the shadows, motioning me in the direction towards the brightly illuminated red exit sign.

"Well, Father Thomas, the name's Elle. I come here every so often, just looking for a good time, if you know what I mean. Say, I used to have a necklace like that when I was younger. My granny gave it to me, but I don't remember what happened to it."

"It was a gift."

The pestilence was nagging me. She continued on without so much as a breath in between. She leaned in, closing the gap between my ear and her lips. I could smell the cheap fragrance reeking from her neck. I stared into the mirror as the outstretched arm slid back into the darkness, still motioning me towards the rear exit.

"I have a confession, Father." She paused and laughed under the sound of the clanking of the bottles and background noise of the pool games.

"Nothing turns me on more than a man in a suit. Why don't we get outta here, grab some of that holy wine, and I'll let you in on some more dark secrets? Whata-ya-say?"

My eyes went from the mirror to my drink, which I quickly grabbed and slid down my throat. I had found my next sacrifice. She was to receive the full extent of punishment for her lust. She was to join the others and bring me closer to the great gates and open arms of our Lord.

"Sure. My truck is parked around back." I stood up, throwing the money on the counter for the drinks. The bartender grabbed up the money and thanked me with a smirk spread across his face.

"Hope she has mercy on you, Father. She's been here a while and left a few empty bottles behind." His tone indicated he knew more than he let on.

We walked around back to the truck and drove off towards the one place I felt was safe to give a lustful sinner her dues: my grandparents' house. My grandmother's health had been declining, and she had since been confined to the local nursing home. Her health was a reflection her age. Barely hanging on but still bound for the glory of Heaven. A saint waiting to be called home.

We pulled up to the house, her hands feeling everywhere and the strong smell of cocktails trailing her breath.

"You'll have to be careful, Father. I'm starting to feel those drinks hit me. Maybe we can go inside for some confessionals?" she spat out in a slur.

We got out and proceeded to the door. I shut the door behind us as she began to look around. Her hand planted on the nearby stove to keep her balance, I reached into the pantry, grabbing the chloroform and dampening the rag. The scuffle was nothing but a brief balancing act, her body falling in on itself as she went limp.

I dragged her dead-weight body to the living room, near the same spot where my grandfather had been found deceased and began to duct-tape her hands and feet. No movement from the soon-to-be lifeless body was a relief. I didn't want to have another blood bath on my hands.

Propping her up into the chair that had held my grandfather all those years before, I sat and waited. I pulled the mask over my head, my breath growing stronger as the anticipation began. The dark doorway soon shifted as one of the figures moved forward, smiling with evil delight.

She began to stir. The towel tied tightly around her head prevented her screams from being heard. I could see the disoriented terror in her bulging eyes. She began to fling herself in every direction, shifting her hands underneath her.

I moved behind her and withdrew the knife I had tucked away in my belt. Her muffled screams mixed with sobbing sniffles grew stronger as I displayed the knife out in front of her. I began to pray for her to be accepted into the arms of her eternal judge. Without warning, her head quickly whipped back, smashing against my face. She reached back with a free hand and ripped the holy symbol of St. Christopher from my neck, flinging it into the shadows of the room.

I managed to gain my composure as she struggled to get her other hand free. Just as she began to pull the gag away to plead or scream, I plunged the knife repeatedly into her neck. The whistle of her begging voice clashed with the gargling of her blood looking for the quickest exit. She held her neck as I thrust the knife in and out of her torso, hoping for the quickest ending possible. The severed artery in her neck continuously sprayed blood into the air, all while I held her head back as she looked into my eyes.

"I'm sorry, Eleanor. I wish I could have been the one to save you, but you abandoned me, just like everyone else!"

I pulled the knife up and then downward, into her eyes, pushing the blade into her skull. The space where her eyes had once been had given way to darkness. I watched in horror while her face and skin slowly subsided to a jet-black appearance. A smile grew across her face. She was now just like them. One of those unwelcomed creatures. Stained with fresh blood, I bolted towards the door and into my car. The drive home was a complete blur. No memory of stop lights. Nothing. Just a darkness I had seen too often.

I awoke half-naked and sitting in frigid water in the tub, my face and hair completely covered with every part of her body. Blood, skin, and brains had all come to rest on me. I sobbed and prayed again for hours and hours, stopping only to crawl out and migrate to my bed. I slowly started to slip away into the deepest of sleeps. Time was no matter now, merely the slave to its master, Death.

#

CHAPTER TWENTY

"He will not grow faint or be discouraged till He has established justice on the earth..." Isaiah 42:4

The knock was loud. It echoed through the hallway into my room. I jumped from the bed, throwing on some clothes and making my way to the door as fast as possible.

"Who is it?"

"It's Detective Gilmour with the Chicago Police Department. Do you have a minute?"

"Sure."

The tension started to rise. I hadn't been gone for more than a day from the scene where I had left Eleanor's body to fester. The blood began to move its way through my body at lightning speed and the hangover coupled with the body aches created a whirlwind of anxiety.

"Come in, Detective. Have a seat. Can I get you anything?"

The detective was trailed by a uniformed officer, both glancing around as they made their way to the couch.

"Nah, that's alright. We shouldn't be too long."

"What can I help you with?" The words flowed from my mouth, awaiting the Miranda Rights to be read.

"Charlie Whipper's work called his parents. Neither of them have seen him for a while. Father Shaun mentioned that you handle services during the week and might have seen him?"

"Now that you mention it, it has been a week or maybe more. He came into service early one morning and then left like usual." I quickly gave them the truth they were looking for.

Detective Gilmour continued to write in a small pocket-sized book while he asked questions.

"Look, Father, there's been a murder and now a missing persons case related to two members of your congregation. Do you know anyone, and I mean anyone, that has been acting suspicious lately? Like not attending when they normally do, staying after service later, or just anything?" The detective and the officer sat staring into my eyes.

"Not that I've noticed. Are you sure it's someone inside the church and not some crazed lunatic looking to get a fix? I've seen some shady characters walk the streets near the church at all hours."

"Unfortunately, we don't have any leads. We were really hoping you would be able to give us something. We appreciate it though. Sorry to bother you, Father." Both of them stood and proceeded through the door.

I stood up and followed them. Without so much as a sound, Detective Gilmour glanced into the bathroom. I moved towards the door to shut it.

"Wait a minute. What's this?" he said as he bent down and grabbed a towel that was stained with blood, picking it up with a pen he had pulled from his pocket. I grabbed it off the pen as a look of extreme concern moved in my direction.

"It was an accident. I smashed my toe the other day and did quite a number. The doctor said it should heal fine. Looks worse than it is." I pointed down at the bandaged area where my small toe had once been.

"Jesus, Father! Sorry. You might get that looked at. You know, it could get infected. We can't have you getting upstairs to the gates too quickly. We might need ya, ya know?" The officer covered his mouth, quietly laughing under his breath.

Detective Gilmour started to step outside the door, pausing to turn with a card in hand. "If you notice anything outta sorts, give me a call. We'll find whoever is doing this. If there's another madman that's on the loose, we gotta find him, and quick. Be careful, Father." He turned and waltzed down the hall.

"Thanks. I'll be in touch." I slammed the door shut, bolting the locks and sliding down the side of the wall.

The fact that the police had made their way to my house drew me into a near panic. I began to scrub the entire bathroom, throwing my clothes into the washer and praying as I moved the scrub brush back and forth across the floor. The urgency of getting everything clean was now of the upmost importance. Cleanliness was going to be the difference between being with my father in Heaven or residing with the tortured souls I had sent to Hell.

I spent the rest of the day in complete isolation, unplugging my phone so as to not be bothered. The bed was the most comfortable I had felt in some time, but it did not last long.

"Father, you have served your superior well. The highest of holiest seeks your continued dedication." The voice echoed from down the dark hallway. A simple shadow darker than its surroundings.

"I already gave you what you wanted! Leave me! I've been obedient. Does that not count for something?"

"Seven. No more, no less."

"Fine! A few more of these and I'm done," I yelled into the twilight.

An uncomfortable laugh permeated the nothingness. I pulled the covers over me and wept.

#

CHAPTER TWENTY-ONE

**"You shall not steal, nor deal falsely, nor lie to one another."
Leviticus 19:11**

I gathered myself that morning in hopes of a moment, even brief, of some actual solitude. The drive into church was quiet. Same with the service. The sermon covered the temptations of Satan and the ability to control oneself in the heat of those moments. The irony was completely lost on the congregation as they received their sacrament of communion. Their agitated and impatient motions were easily ignored. I knew what lay ahead for those that wished to not practice the gospel that had been given.

Taking off my robe afterwards, I sat down to fulfill the additional administrative duties that had been transferred to me after the untimely demise of Mrs. Belfort, when Father Shaun entered.

"Great sermon today, Thomas." He reached to shake my hand with a firm grip.

"Thank you. I feel like I am coming back into focus after all the illness that's plagued me recently."

He nodded with a smile across his face. "Did Detective Gilmour happen stop by? He brought up the Whipper boy, said he was missing. I told him you might have heard something. You can't tell with that kid. He's a hard one to pin down. Probably ran away or something."

"Yeah, that's what I figured happened. I haven't seen him in quite a while."

"Well, I hope they find him. I've added him to the prayer list this week. Don't forget to keep Margie in your prayers as well. Still no word on her murder. I'm not sure the Lord will be so kind to forgive the ruthless monster that did that to her."

"What do you mean, Father?" I stared with great curiosity.

"Whoever did that was either unstable or a practicing Satanist. You know how those cults are now-a-days. It seems they just pop up outta nowhere. They sacrifice the innocent and leave nothing behind. Cold-blooded with no remorse."

"Why do you think she was innocent?" I asked under my breath.

"Excuse me?" Father Shaun asked, double-checking he had heard correctly.

"Nothing, Father."

"Alright. Let me know if you hear anything. Oh, and another thing, where's your crest of St. Christopher? I don't remember a day you didn't wear it."

The immediate panic must have flashed across my face. I had forgotten that it had been dislodged from my neck in the scuffle with Eleanor. A blank stare had certainly appeared across my face as I searched for an explanation. An explanation to such a mundane question now turning into a crisis in the confines of my head.

"Oh, yes. I...I took it to get cleaned. It was starting to show some tarnish."

"Gotcha. Be safe out there, Thomas. Glad you're feeling better. Don't let the stress of providing eternal salvation get to ya." He laughed as he closed the door behind him.

Jumping up from my seat, I rushed to grab my keys. I had to retrieve the necklace, or I would not sleep well, or at all. There are instances in one's life where urgency was a never-fleeting shadow that followed you. This was one of those instances.

\#

CHAPTER TWENTY-TWO

"Search me, O God, and know my heart; try me and know my anxious thoughts." Psalm 139:23-24

There were only mere hours left of daylight, so I quietly waited in the nearby liquor store parking lot. The sounds of each clanking bottle rattled me to my very core. Tense sensations and anxious sweats only served to feed a defeated mood. I had been protected by those that called me into service for so long. Surely, they would continue to do so in my own forgetfulness. Lights on the front of the store flickered on, signaling that the time was near. I slowly pulled away from the neon-lit parking lot and traversed the short drive of two blocks at a moderate pace. I could not bring any attention to myself.

I made the decision to return to my grandparents' house after the streetlights had kicked on. The neighborhood was desolate and not many residents lived in the area nowadays. This was why it was a prime location to punish future transgressors. The door creaked open as the stench of rotting and decaying flesh made me nearly gag. She was merely a vessel, returning to the black hole she had come from. From the darkness, into the darkness.

I wrapped my handkerchief over my nose and mouth and began to scour the room in search of my most coveted necklace. I had searched every inch of the hardwood covered room, tiptoeing over the pool of blood that lay beneath Eleanor's body. Nothing. There was no sign of the crest that had protected me for so long.

Pulling out one of the few vintage yellow dining chairs still surrounding the aluminum framed table, I could feel defeat. The heat of the summer evening and the immense stress brought on a near violent sweat, the beads of water flowing and tapping against the table top in a syncopated beat while my hands drew up into my face. It had to be there. Eleanor had thrown it violently, but the room contained very little that could hide it from sight. My breath holding as an icy aura filled the room.

"We never left!"

The loud whisper in my ear nearly threw me from my chair. Startled, I surveyed the room to see who had fluttered my eardrums.

"What more do you want? I gave you what you asked for. Leave me alone," I begged as I continued to scan every foot of the kitchen.

"Long time, no see, Father! You look a little confused."

My eyes bulged from my head as I gripped the seat beneath me, the beating of my heart now audible to my own ears as it pounded like a bass drum playing its final notes.

"Relax, Father. I'm not going to hurt you. By the way, you look nervous. How about some water?"

An ice-cold cup of water slid across the table, leaving a path on the dusty tabletop.

"Char...lie Whipper? How is this possible?" The heavy breathing had dried everything in my mouth and chapped my lips.

"How am I here? How am I alive? Well, see, that's the thing. I'm not. Remember?"

The shaking in my hands. The intense shaking. It travelled through my body as the urge to run fought against the selfish need to understand.

"This isn't real. This is some..."

"Shut the fuck up, Father! You know why I'm here and I know why you're here. You honestly think that we would go quietly? You think that you would be the one to send us to Hell? Well, guess what? Hell has no vacancies." Charlie's tone grew into a quick rage.

I sat, unnerved, as I looked at the figure claiming to be Charlie Whipper. His throat with a large gaping wound that appeared like an endless black hole where his soul had once been. The white shirt he had been wearing the evening of the event, covered in coagulated blood and stained with his sins.

"What do you mean, us?" My feeling of confusion quickly turned to horror as I watched Margie Belfort and Eleanor shift out of the darkness behind Charlie. "You were all sinners. I had no choice. You were called by God's will!" I screamed out at the disfigured and soulless beings before me.

Charlie laughed while a small trickle of blood ran from the wound in his neck. "You think you get to decide what's right and what's wrong? Let me tell you something, Father, we're never going to leave now. You put us here. We are staying here. We're with you always now."

The cloud of confusion quickly began to defuse.

"Purgatory?" I asked.

He nodded his head and smiled. I could see the sinister look as his face nearly resembled those that had called them to their doom.

"I'm not feeling well. I'm gonna go." I began to stand, trying to gather my thoughts as my stomach slowly began to crawl up into my mouth.

"You wouldn't wanna leave without your protection, would you? See, we know why you came back. You know why you came back. And the police, they will know why you came back, won't they?" Charlie chuckled as he opened his palm. The necklace dangling with the crest of St. Christopher rested in his palm.

"It's a real shame, Tommy boy. You're going to tell us why you did what you did and maybe we can work something out, okay?" He clasped his hand shut, the emblem surrounded by his palm.

I nodded. There was no escape from this. They had been sent to the holding for eternal judgement, and I was now at their mercy.

"You committed the sins that were unforgiveable. The transgressions that only bring eternal damnation. You all three broke the covenant you had with God. The seven deadly sins. All are damned." I was stern in my words. They knew what they had done.

"Well, Father Thomas, you've put yourself in quite a pickle. See, your unmerciful slaughter led you to commit one of these sins as well. Wrath. So, do yourself a favor and turn yourself in. It's only a matter of time before you join us in this desolate existence. Maybe, just maybe, God will grant you a special council with him. Maybe turning yourself in will cancel out some of shitty things you did in this life. Probably not, though."

Charlie slid the pendant across the table, and I immediately grabbed it up.

"Go to Hell!" I screamed at them as they started to laugh.

"We'll see you soon, Father," Charlie said as his face shifted forms into one of the dark beings that had been summoning me. My jaw hung in horror. It smiled and pointed in my direction its arm growing in length as it looked to reach out for me. I drew my knife. The same one that had sent all those that deserved it to their final resting place.

The sound of footsteps outside suddenly echoed throughout the house. Banging on the door of the aging home rang out and pierced the silence within.

"Chicago Police Department! Open the fucking door!" I could hear Detective Gilmour scream out as the door unexpectedly was thrown open. Uniforms filled the room with their guns drawn. Point-blank. In my direction.

"Freeze! Put the knife down." Detective Gilmour stood shaking, gripping his gun with both hands.

"Thomas, do what they say. We will work this out. All will be forgiven," Father Shaun, standing behind the police, shouted.

I gripped the knife as the uniforms slowly gave way to the creatures that had come for me, their guns dripping black ooze and then changing shape into long, extended arms, motioning at me. They would never let me go. They were restless. Their appetites unsatiated. My faith had been committed, and these demons were to be exorcised. Holding my protection in one hand, I drew the knife back with the other and lunged forward.

Forgive them, for they know not what they do.

There was no pain. Just a thousand flashes of light. A collapse into a murky nonexistence. From the darkness, and into the darkness, I came, and I returned.

\#

CHAPTER TWENTY-THREE

"I will bear the indignation of the Lord because I have sinned against him, until he pleads my cause and executes judgment for me. He will bring me forth to the light; I shall behold his deliverance." Micah 7:9

"Hello, Father. Pleasant surprise seeing you here."

A voice echoing through the abyss. A dim light that grew greater in strength, washing into a color scheme that felt all too familiar. I felt nothing. No anger, rage, or happiness. Just being. My sight slowly adjusting and focusing on a gray concrete wall in front of me. Jolting up in panic, I found myself standing in the most familiar of places.

"Go ahead and sit down. You're going to be here for a long while." His voice was subtle yet stern.

"Alex? Alex Fulmer? What happened? Where am I?" The questions began to fall drop from my mouth as I felt my face and clothing. I could feel it all.

"I don't know why or how, but you're here. You're not going any-where anytime soon either. I've seen it before and probably will again," Alex said as he turned from staring at the dull cement wall in front of him.

"Am I in prison? I don't know what happened."

His eyes became fixated on mine, like a carnivore waiting to shred meat from the bone. The certainty in his gaze spoke volumes about the reality, or lack thereof.

"You're awaiting trial. Just like the others before and the others after. You see, I'm confined to a cell till they cook me. Then, I'll be sitting right beside you. We're not so different, you and me. We both submitted to our urges. The urge to make right what we thought was wrong. I got caught, and you got cooked. No one else sees you. No one else can. We exist on the same plane of being, but in different forms. Get what I mean?"

I stared into that fine-grain cement wall. I knew exactly what he meant.

"I'm dead?"

Alex began to laugh to himself. "Not really dead, but not alive either. Tell me something? What is it that got you here in this predica-ment? Please tell me it's not the same reason they locked those other priests up in isolation. I'd hate to drag that hammer along till I got to Hell, Father."

"No. Not at all. I was simply following the commandments of God. Returning the old bastards to the fire from which they crawled. I was just doing the Lord's work."

Alex began laughing hysterically. "Me, too. Me, too. I guess we both are gonna get what we deserve, huh?" His laugh broke into a more serious tone.

"Don't worry though. You won't be alone. Trust me, you're never alone," he said as the light from the exterior windows became obstructed by shadows.

Standing outside the cell were the figures of my mother, Charlie Whipper, Margie Belfort, and Eleanor. I stood up, backing myself against the wall. Eleanor opened her hand and displayed the St. Christopher pendant in her palm.

"They're waiting for your turn, Father. They wait every day. They'll wait for eternity, if they have to."

Their stares, burning holes through me, warned of the unspeakable horrors that awaited me.

"I gave them the forgiveness they pleaded for when God would not entertain their requests. Their beginning and endings were all the same. From the darkness, into the darkness. It was His will. My will."

THE END.

ACKNOWLEDGEMENTS

Dedicated to my loving and supportive family and friends who never question my weird side but openly embrace it.

Stay Weird. It's ok.

ABOUT THE AUTHOR

Currently nestled between cornfields and the majestic Wabash River in southern Indiana, James Watjen spends his days honing his craft as a writer and filmmaker while cherishing precious moments with his wife and three wonderful children.

His journey as a storyteller has been deeply influenced by a lifelong fascination with the thriller and horror genres, with masters of the craft like Stephen King, George Romero, and William Lustig serving as the backbone of his inspiration. It's from this talented and amazing group of storytellers that he draws his greatest inspirations. Whether it be through the classic novels of King or the psychological and unhinged works of Romero and Lustig, the influence is sometimes subtle yet present.

James is currently working through several original and disturbing releases for the next few years